BEYOND

THE VALLEY OF SEX AND SHOPPING

E. P. ROSE

TA13LE

Beyond the Valley of Sex and Shopping, E. P. Rose

Published 2012
Table Thirteen Books
94 Church Road
Barnes
London
SW13 0DQ

ISBN: 978-0-9571507-4-4

Cover & book design by The Art Partnership Ltd
Typeset by SRA Books
Printed by TJ International, Cornwall, UK

CONTENTS

1

STEALING THUNDER

Being The First Part Of The Second Most Horrible Day In Jennifer Perry's Life

Making that first step up required every ounce of the Porge's far from ample store of courage. From where he was standing, the top of the frame seemed a long, a very long way up.

But, if he was going to slide down the slide, like Suzie and Anton and Tom, this was a climb he was going to have to make.

In so far as someone who is not quite two can affect nonchalance, the Porge affected it, and proceeded to ascend – whereupon his toes began to tingle with the beginnings of a smile of incipient accomplishment, which was due to reach his face round about the time he reached the top, if he ever did, and illuminate it.

Tom, who was freckled and four and lived next door, lay on his front in the paddling pool. His chin was in the water. When he rippled the water with his fingers, the sunlight flashed and danced. He opened his mouth.

"Don't drink the water, Tom," said the real Mary Poppins. She gave him a look over the top of the latest Agatha Christie.

"I'm not eating the water," said Tom, "I'm eating the light."

"You can eat as much light as you want, Tom, provided you don't drink the water, which is full of germs and will probably make you sick. And I shouldn't be at all surprised if your stomach didn't blow up and you exploded all over the garden and it took us two weeks to pick up the pieces and put them in a brown paper bag."

This gave Tom something to think about, while Mary Poppins returned her attention to "A Murder Is Announced", which had been given to her as a birthday present by Felix and Jennifer Perry, her employers, and the parents of Suzie and the Porge. There was an inscription in the front: "To Mary Poppins. With best wishes from all the Perrys. Very many happy returns of the day. June 19. 1950."

"I read in the paper, Mary," Mrs.Perry had said, "that Agatha Christie is Mr Attlee's favourite author."

"Good God," Mr Perry had failed to refrain from snorting. "And people wonder why this country's going to the dogs."

Mary Poppins turned the page.

Designed and built by Mr Perry, with tender loving care and not a moment's thought for the future of the planet's non-replaceable trees (this being pre-all that), the climbing frame was an excellent construction. It featured not only the laddery bit, which the Porge was presently ascending, and the platform at the top, to which the top of the slide was attached, but also a monkey-run and a swing.

On the swing sat Suzie, golden sun-kissed daredevil Sue, swinging gently back and forth, in her spiffing gingham swim-suit with the frill around the bum, scuffling her bare toes in the warm and dusty landing strip, surveying the scene through squinty eyes against the glare, and calculating trajectories and velocities and the like, with what can only be described as a calculating look upon her beautiful four year old face.

The swing swung from North to South. Tom, in the North, in the paddling-pool, attempting to approach his bottom lip to within a nano-millimeter of the surface and suck the sunlight in, was in range.

But so was Tom's friend, Anton, in the sandpit, in the South. And Anton was building a sandcastle, the scope and sophistication of which belied his three and three-quarter years.

Suzie pulled herself up by the ropes to stand on the seat of the swing, just as the proud and beaming Porge made it onto the platform and announced, pronouns still being problematic: "My climbed up!"

Suzie glared at her brother with unconcealed disdain and hissed: "Don't talk to me, Porge, I'm busy."

She lowered herself into position, facing South. To leap from the swing to the sandpit and flatten Anton's castle. Irresistible.

As Suzie set herself in motion, the Porge edged his way around the platform and came to the top of the slide. From where he was standing now, at the top of the slide, the bottom looked a long, a very long way down. He lowered his dear little bottom onto the platform, so that his dear little legs pointed down the slide. Holding onto the edge, his dear little knuckles were white.

Suzie's arc of swing was one hundred and seventy-eight. She was one degree off the horizontal.

The Porge plucked all his little courage up.

"Look at me, Mary Poppins!" cried the Porge – and pushed off.

"Look at me, Mary Poppins!" cried the Suze – and let go.

Mary Poppins came out of the closet in which Miss Marple was hiding, waiting to trap the murderer, too late to do anything but gawp, as Suzie sailed through the air, squealing with delight.

Give the girl ten out of ten for accuracy. She flattened Anton's sandcastle good and proper. But the landing was lousy. First she broke her ankle. Then she pitched sideways onto her shoulder and fractured her collar-bone.

The fictional Mary Poppins would, doubtless, have intervened in some sort of epiphenomenal way – and have saved the day by, for example, flouting the laws of gravity. The real Mary Poppins, however, having been born in Bromley, and not in the mind of a writer of children's fiction, was gravitationally conventional. She operated in accordance with the laws of first aid, then went inside to use the telephone.

Beautiful Jennifer Perry was half naked and halfway to Guildford, incommunicado in a hotel room, where she was coming to breathless terms with a penis, which did not belong to her husband.

Dutiful Felix Perry, her husband, was hard at work in his office in Birdcage Walk, attempting to come to terms with the economic implications of the deployment of American ground troops in South Korea, when the call came through.

Susan Perry was coming to terms with pain, and showing true grit.

But the Porge was failing to come to terms at all.

Oh, the gloriousness of that first descent – down and down and down the slippery slide, not the least part of which was anticipation of that delicious moment when he would share his triumph with a wildly cheering and warmly appreciative audience.

And oh, the bitterness of his disappointment, as he slid to a giddy gleeful halt, only to hear his sister's scream and only to see that no-one was paying him the tiniest blind bit of notice.

He was too young to rejoice in another's pain, having no concept of pain in anyone other than himself. And his grip on the language was far too slight to put into words the feelings that tore him asunder.

The look on his face, though, said it just right:

"That bitch just stole my thunder."

2

STRAIGHT UP - WITH A BEE

Being The Second Part
Of The Second Most Horrible Day
In Jennifer Perry's Life

The penis, referred to in the previous chapter, was attached to Tom's dad, Hugo Foster-Wilson.

The Perrys and the Foster-Wilsons were neighbours, at numbers nine and eleven, respectively.

In common with the Prime Minister and Mary Poppins, Caroline Foster-Wilson, Hugo's wife and mother of Tom, was tucked up in bed with "A Murder Is Announced". She had a pretty shrewd idea whodunnit, but as to her husband's passion for the woman who lived next door – not a clue.

In the nursery at Number Eleven, Tom was asleep and dreaming of sunlight sandwiches.

In the nursery at Number Nine, which he shared with his temporarily hospitalised sister, the Porge was supposed to be asleep, but his eyes were open wide and staring at the bars of his cot. Suzie had been out of her cot before she was one. The Porge, however, had never shown the slightest inclination to escape. Until tonight. Tonight was different. Things had changed. He'd scaled the heights of the climbing frame. He had slid down the slide. He had experienced powerful emotions.

The night was hot, and the moon was full.

In the children's ward, kept in for observation, Suzie Perry ground her teeth and whimpered in her sleep.

Jennifer Perry looked at her daughter and groaned and hit herself hard on her head with her fist.

A girlfriend of hers had once opined in low and conspiratorial tones:

"The thing about extra-marital sex, my dear, is that when it's bad, it's awful – but when it's good, it's worse."

When Jennifer Perry considered Hugo and herself in that hotel room halfway to Guildford, and the afternoon's heroic feats of sexual derring-do, she suddenly knew what it was that girlfriend of hers had been on about. And she hit herself again, drawing blood this time with the diamond ring that dear kind Felix had bought for her from Wartski's of Llandudno.

She would never hurt Felix. He was a wonderful husband, a wonderful father – and if it were not for this afternoon, she would never have known that he wasn't a wonderful lover. But now she knew. Felix wasn't, and Hugo was – quite marvellous. And could she bear never to have him inside her again?

She burst into tears.

The little girl awoke.

"Mummy?"

"Shush."

"It hurts."

"Go back to sleep."

On the hand that stroked her daughter's brow, the blood-stained diamond picked up all the moonbeams in the room.

Mary Poppins finished her book and her cocoa, switched off the bedside light and fell asleep. It had not occurred to her to feel in any way awkward about being left alone in the house with dear kind Felix. He was not that sort of man.

In the nursery, the Porge's little fists closed around the bars of his cot. He proceeded to haul himself up.

Dear kind Felix fixed himself another gin martini, straight up with an olive, and wandered out onto the moonlit terrace. He sighed with contentment. He was fifty. He was large. A benign armadillo of a man in a pin-stripe suit.

There was something to be said for marrying late. He was settled. He was secure. He could take things in his amiable armadillo stride. He had perspective. That was it. Perspective. When accidents occurred, he had the wherewithal to put them right. And he could see things for what they were. Of course, he hated the idea of his child in pain. But the pain would pass. Broken bones mend, and childhood's golden summer would resume.

He smiled and sipped his drink and stepped off the terrace onto the moonlit lawn, a satisfied man, blissfully ignorant of the passions that seethed on the other side of the garden wall, beneath the Foster-Wilson's fine magnolia tree.

There, under that lovely tree, sat Hugo, smoking in the dark – lean, young, handsome and longing for more of Jennifer Perry. He held his breath at the sound of his neighbour's brogues on the terrace next door. The last thing he wanted was speech with the man who stood between him and his heart's desire. Because, if he spoke to him, he would tell him, and then where would he be? It was all so unfair. He should never have married Caroline, who would have been far better off married to Felix instead, leaving Jennifer free for endless days and nights of passion with him. Not that there was anything wrong with Caroline. There was not. She was, in fact, perfectly pleasant. She was a good mother, an attentive wife. But where was the .... sexual splendour?

The Porge climbed out of his cot.

Bravo!

He toddled over to the nursery door, crossed the landing and went into Mary Poppins' room. He stood by her bed, quiet as a mouse, and watched her sleep. Then he came out of her room and went to the top of the stairs.

"But on the other hand," thought Hugo Foster-Wilson, "why the hell not? Why not just go up to him and put it to him straight: calmly, rationally, man to man. 'Now, look here old chap, this wife business. Obviously been a bit of a mix up. You and Jennifer. Me and Caroline. Don't know how it happened. Obviously ought to be the other way around. So let's be brave. Let's be modern. Let's be forward thinking. Let's not have any more of this furtive secret hotel stuff. I don't want to cuckold you, my friend. Let's get it all out in the open. Let's swap. Any objections?"

From the top of the house to the bottom, there were four flights of stairs. The Porge came down them feet first on his tummy.

"And pigs might fly," thought Hugo with a sigh.

"Hugo."

It was Caroline, calling to her husband from their bedroom's casement window.

"Come to bed."

"How lovely she looks in the moonlight," thought Felix, hidden from view at the children's end of the garden.

Then he heard the sound of Hugo crunching across gravel, doors being shut. A husband and wife retiring to bed. Very nice.

Felix finished his drink, but postponed the ultimate pleasure of the olive, and placed the still chilled glass upon the platform of the climbing frame. He ran his hand over the wood, which he had sanded and polished for days before declaring it to be safe and splinter-free. He looked at the full moon, reflected in the waters of the paddling pool. This was a beautiful sight. Felix could hardly believe sometimes how much there was in the world to give him pleasure.

Something flew across the moon.

Near or far? Small or large? Felix could not say.

It was a late-night bee, which landed on his olive.

Felix licked his lips, anticipating the olive, and swept up his glass with a flourish.

When antigen is injected into the bloodstream, as happens with a bee or wasp sting, it spreads rapidly to large numbers of mast cells all over the body; and this results in the simultaneous discharge of very large quantities of histamine. The resulting symptoms – a condition called anaphylactic shock – are explosive and dramatic. Within a minute or two, weals develop all over the skin. Because the tissue round the face is soft, it can swell easily; and the tissue round the eyes may become so puffy that within minutes or so the eyes may close completely. The lips swell up, and the throat feels thick, due to swelling of tissue round the tongue and mouth. The wholesale inflammation of the skin causes a massive drop in blood pressure, so that the victim develops a rapid heartbeat, and may actually faint.

Felix, stung in the throat, was choking too. He staggered about quite a bit, and when he did actually faint, it was, mercifully, just prior to pitching forward into the paddling pool, splashing into the moon, where he drowned.

The Porge traversed the drawing room, passed through the conservatory, and out onto the terrace.

The York stone was still warm to his slipperless feet.

The grass was cool.

When he reached his Dad, face down in the paddling pool, with the moon's reflection reassembling itself over his head, he paused for the briefest moment to ponder this latest example of adult eccentricity, before making a detour round the outflung legs, the well-shod feet, heading for the climbing frame's first rung.

And up he went, without a pause.

"Dad, look at me, Dad. Dad, look at me."

But he was not particularly surprised when his father did not reply. It was typical. Typical.

Nothing daunted, down the slide the little monkey came.

And up he went.

And down he came. A dozen times – which was excellent fun – until he became tired and bored and went back inside. Up the stairs. Back into his cot. His head hit the pillow. Instantly asleep. And no one would ever know how, on the night his father died, George the Porge went up and down the slide.

Just before midnight, Mary Poppins woke up, pulled on her dressing gown, slipped into her slippers, checked on her charge and went downstairs, where she found the lights on and the doors into garden open.

Subsequently she found Felix and, having ascertained that he was well beyond first aid, that he was cold, went inside and made the appropriate calls.

3

THE RINGS OF SATAN

Mary Poppins, née Clarke, was no stranger to sudden and violent death.

Mind you, this could be said of any other human on the planet.

Arithmetic tells us that if all the Second World War's fifty-five million dead were laid end to end, they would circle the earth some 15.67 times.

In certain astronomical circles, these astronomical circles are called The Rings of Satan.

They touched everyone. Some more than others.

Norman Clarke, Mary's father, was on duty in Croydon. A German bomb dropped out of the sky and blew him to kingdom come.

Ernest Clarke, her older brother, was on duty in the sky, the Libyan sky. Italian anti-aircraft fire blew him to kingdom come.

Vincent Clarke, her younger brother, went to war in Burma, stepped on a Japanese mine, and was blown to kingdom come.

Come the war's end, when for a loopy moment it seemed as though the killing had to stop, Mary Clarke took the plunge and married the man she loved. His name was Martin – Martin Patrick Reginald Poppins. He was, as her father had been, a policeman.

Her marriage to Martin took Mary into realms of happiness she never knew existed. They were in love. It was perfect. It was good. And when she conceived, it was better.

Then the powers that be decided to send Sergeant Martin

Poppins to Palestine, which was where the Stern Gang blew him up.

Mary lost the baby.

Then her Uncle Peter, her mother's brother, who had come through the conflict unscathed, was crushed to death at Burden Park, the Bolton Wanderers' ground, after thousands of supporters broke down fencing to get into a packed enclosure to watch the FA Cup-tie with Stoke City.

For Mary's mother, Prudence Clarke, this was the final straw. She took to her bed, suffering from, if anything, terminal incredulity.

Mary Poppins nursed her till she died some two years later.

After the funeral, leafing through the paper in a hopeless kind of way, she happened to espy, in Situations Vacant, the following announcement:

MARY POPPINS REQUIRED
For two year old Susan
and nought year old George.

What with one thing and another, it seemed to Mary, the Widow Poppins, that this was very much more than likely to be the perfect position for her.

And so it was.

For Mary, Number Nine was a shelter, a haven, safe water after the storm – it was Howard's End. It was home. And she loved it. She loved her little room under the eaves, across the landing from the nursery, and the bathroom she shared with the children. She loved the peace of it, the routine of it, the safeness. (Hah!)

But most of all she loved the Porge.

Suzie, from the off, was a self-contained little girl. You couldn't cuddle Suzie in the way that you could cuddle the

Porge. She was like an arrow, zinging towards some distant bull's-eye. Suzie did not require affection. What she needed was the thrill of flight.

4

THE END OF THE AFFAIR

The sudden departure of Felix to that great Foreign Office in the sky was not, ostensibly, so greatly felt by the children. They were too young. For them, Felix had always been a distant and somewhat daunting figure, glimpsed at breakfast and at bedtime. Let's face it. Felix Perry was a middle-aged, middle-class mandarin, absolutely typical of his species in his almost pathological inability to express any kind of feeling or emotion with anything more physically extravagant than a handshake.

This is not to say that he did not have feelings, that he did not, in fact, seethe with all manner of powerful emotions. Look at the climbing-frame. This humble structure was a veritable monument to paternal affection, and love was the glue which held it together. The climbing-frame was Felix Perry's Taj Mahal – but the children never knew. They accepted it as their due, the way that children do.

Jennifer knew.

Remember Klaus Fuchs?

He was the German-born Communist scientist, who had been working at the Hartwell weapons research centre in Berkshire, when he was arrested for passing on atomic secrets to the Russians.

The Foster-Wilsons and the Perrys had been dining together at the Ivy and, over the coffee and cognac, the subject of Fuchs had come up.

"So, Felix," said Hugo, "about this mystery woman – any inside info?"

"Which mystery woman is that, my dear fellow?"

"The one that MI5 is hunting down, the one who spent weekends of passion with Fuchs."

He rhymed it with ducks – and enjoyed his wife's discomfort as she blushed into her cup.

"I don't think I could quite imagine a weekend of passion with him," said Jennifer, giving Hugo a look, which led him, for the first time, to begin to imagine a weekend of passion with her.

A waiter with a coffee-pot appeared, poured and withdrew.

Not unferociously, Caroline opined:

"I think that he should have been hanged."

"I'm not so sure," said Felix, "that treason is always a capital crime."

"I should jolly well think it was," said Hugo.

"Supposing you had access to secrets," said Felix, "and the agents of some unscrupulous foreign power approached you and put a gun to your head and demanded that you hand them over."

"I should tell the foreign fiends to pull the bally trigger."

"Of course you should," said Felix. "So should I. But suppose, instead, they put a gun to Caroline's head and demand that you hand the secrets over then – or else. Then what would you do?"

"I should hope," said the staunch Caroline, "that Hugo would not hesitate to do his duty."

"That's my girl," said Hugo.

"Your country or your wife. What would you do, darling?" asked Jennifer quietly.

"I think, I'm afraid, it would depend on the nature of the secrets involved."

"How do you mean?"

"If I knew for a fact that sparing your life would mean the

death of, say, a thousand innocent others, I .... I'm not sure that I know what I'd do."

"I'm sure you'd do what's right," said Jennifer, with an edge of primness in her voice.

"I do know, however," said Felix, "that if they threatened my children's life, no matter how many innocents be damned, I'd give the buggers anything they want. And if they hang me for it, well, so be it."

Jennifer looked at her husband, in the somewhat embarrassed silence that greeted this speech, and realised that what he had just made was a curiously roundabout declaration of love for his children – and that he loved them more than his country, more than his life and, effectively, more than her.

Felix excused himself, pushed back his chair and ambled off in the direction of the bar, where, with typical discretion, he planned to settle the bill away from the table.

Caroline, then, went to powder her nose.

Hugo and Jennifer, left alone at the table, watched their respective spouses out of sight. They were suddenly self-conscious, were silent, then started both to speak at once.

"You first," said she.

"If you were my wife ......" he began, and looked into her marvellous eyes and was lost in them.

"Yes?"

"What?"

"If I was your wife ......?" she prompted.

"The rest of the world could go hang."

The funny thing was, though, that as soon as Felix died, Hugo changed his tune.

Jennifer engineered the second tryst. She had tickets for Frank Sinatra's London debut concert at the London Palladium. Felix had bought them.

"Do you think it would be wrong of me to go?" she asked

Caroline, over the garden wall. "I can't help thinking it's what Felix would have wanted."

"You must do what you think is right, my dear? Do you want to go?"

"Yes. For Felix. Yes."

"Then you must go. It'll do you good. And Hugo will take you – won't you, dearest?"

"Won't I what?" asked Hugo, who was sitting in a deckchair at the time, reading his paper, enjoying the July sun and the prospect of the imminent end of soap rationing.

"Take Jennifer to the Frank Sinatra concert."

"I can't stand Frank Sinatra," Hugo opined. "Dreadful little man."

"You can jolly well stand him for one night."

Of course, they did not go to the concert. They went to a small hotel, where Jennifer removed her clothes and laid on the bed.

Hugo sat down on a chair, put his head in his hands and groaned.

"What's the matter?" she asked.

"It's no good," he replied.

"What do you mean?"

"I can't do it. I'm sorry."

"You mean," said Jennifer, with breath-taking acuity, "that it's alright to fuck a man's wife when he's alive, but it's not alright to fuck a man's wife when he's dead."

Hugo flinched. He dwindled.

Jennifer got up off the bed and reached for her stockings.

He watched her through the fingers which covered his face. Neither spoke.

Needless to say, it was hopelessly sexy, watching her put her clothes back on. By the time Jennifer was once again dressed, all of his scruples had flown out of the window, and he had, in Henry Miller's immortal locution, an erection fit to break a plate. But it was too late.

She looked at him, shook her head and sighed.

"Come on," she said. "Let's go."

They went to the London Palladium and caught the end of the show.

And that was the end of that.

They never spoke of it again.

5

WETTING THE BED

Because his father had withdrawn moral support in the most complete way – by dying.

Because he was insecure and too easily convinced that he was inadequate.

Because he was afraid to compete with other boys or to stand up to them.

Because he was inclined to feel dominated by his mother.

Because he was too strictly brought up to fight back openly.

Because he was jealous of his sister.

Because he had bad dreams.

Because he was scared at the thought of going away to boarding school at the age of six.

The Porge's night-time problems with his bladder represented something of a mini-boom for a whole generation of paediatricians and child psychologists, each one of whom had a different theory as to the cause and a different proposal as to the cure.

Certainly, his father was dead, but whether or not this was the reason he wet the bed – who could say?

Certainly, he was insecure, but that was because he wet the bed.

Certainly, he was afraid of other boys, but that was because he was scared they would find out that he wet the bed.

Certainly, he felt that his mother was disappointed in him, because he wet the bed.

Certainly, he was jealous of his sister, because, apart from anything else, she did not wet the bed.

Certainly, he had bad dreams, in which he wet the bed.

And certainly, he was scared of going away to boarding school at the age of six, because he wet the fucking bed.

If Felix had been alive, when he was six, there would have been no discussion. The Porge would have been packed off to Hindhead, for which his name had been down since he was born, and that would have been that. St. Edmund's, Hindhead. Then Stowe. It was all arranged. Father's footsteps. But then, if Felix had been alive, maybe the Porge would not have wet his bed. Who knows?

Jennifer tended to concur with Dr Moet of Harley Street:

"In my opinion, Mrs Perry, you should send your son away to school, because this will remove him from the competitive arena of his home, in which he is clearly overshadowed by his over-achieving older sister, and will provide him with just the dramatic change of circumstance needed to cure him of his affliction."

"What nonsense," said Mary Poppins, whose relationship with Jennifer had developed considerably over the last four years, "the Porge loves Susan. He'd miss her terribly."

Mary Poppins sided with Dr Chandon of Wigmore Place in his view that many children wet the bed quite naturally even up to their thirteenth year and, given the circumstances, it would simply be a cruelty to send the boy away.

"And let's face it," said Mary, "you'd miss him terribly, too – and so would I."

This was an understatement. Mary Poppins dreaded the thought of sending him off.

"I only want to do what's best for the boy," Jennifer persisted, with the ghost of her husband breathing down her neck. "Apart from which, we've left it so late. Where else could he go?"

"St.Anthony's, in Hampstead, where Tom's friend, Anton, goes. It's an excellent school – and I happen to know that Anton's friend, Ollie, won't be going back next term, because his father is moving the family back to Toronto – so there's a place."

Mary Poppins was on the case. Jennifer Perry felt her resolve dissolve and reached for a cigarette, despite the fact that the British Standing Advisory Committee on cancer and chemotherapy had only just that week announced that a relationship between smoking and lung cancer had to be regarded as established.

Mary Poppins took him on the bus to Daniel Neale's, where she bought him a smart blue blazer and cap with a bright green eagle on it – and he went to St.Anthony's, where Tom's friend, Anton, took great pleasure in calling him "The Porge" and in making sure that the other boys did so too – and he continued to wet the bed.

In the year that Frank Lloyd Wright and Buddy Holly died, and John McEnroe was born, and two monkeys called Able and Baker went into space and returned, Suzie was thirteen and went off to Benenden, thereby removing herself from the competitive home arena, at least during term time – and the Porge still wet his bed, setting off the electric bell, which was attached to a rubber pad, placed beneath his easily washable, fitted polyester sheet.

He stuck with that ridiculous contraption for over a year, but it did no good.

Stowe?

Jennifer tried to persuade him to go.

"I won't," said the Porge.

"Your father said the happiest years of his life were spent at Stowe."

"I don't care."

"Georgie, darling ....."

"I'm not going."
"But why?" she cried, knowing full well.
"Because I'm an incontinent cretin and I have no desire to be persecuted by a bunch of boarding school bullies."
"Darling, you are not a cretin."
"I'm thirteen years old and I wet my bed!"
To follow Tom's friend, Anton, to a day school, to St. Paul's, in the certain knowledge that Anton would make sure that everyone called him "The Porge", was the lesser of two evils.
And that's where he went – to St. Paul's.
And the Sixties unfolded, one soggy sheet at a time.
Suzie got nine O-levels – to the Porge's paltry five.
She played hockey and tennis for the school, took the lead in plays and was president of the debating society. Princess Anne and the other younger girls looked up to her. She discovered sex and succeeded in persuading Mary Poppins, who was at that time enduring with stoic aplomb the embarrassment of Julie Andrews' Oscar-winning "Mary Poppins" film, to arrange for her to go on the pill (without telling Jennifer) – and then proceeded, with enormous vigour and gusto, to notch up sexual conquests by the score. Indeed, if sex had been an official sport at the Tokyo Olympics, Susan Perry would have been captain of the squad – and she would have brought home gold for Britain in every single event.
The Porge went to Harrods on the bus and spent his pocket-money on three white mice in the pet department there.
"Oh God," groaned Mary Poppins, when he brought them home, "not mice."
"You're not to think of them as pets, Mary," explained the patient Porge. "You're to think of them as medicine."
"What are you talking about?"
"It's Pliny the Elder's idea, actually. You boil up mice and eat them and it cures you of wetting the bed."

"You can tell your nasty friend that he's talking through his hat."

"I can't."

"Oh yes you can – and you can take the beastly things back where they came from. I don't want them here when your mother comes home."

"I can't, because Pliny the Elder, is not, as you fondly seem to imagine, a boy at my school. Pliny the Elder, Mary, is dead."

"Oh. Well, I'm not surprised."

"He died of fumes and exhaustion while investigating the eruption of Vesuvius in A.D.79."

"Well, I'm glad to see you're learning something at last."

Then she drove him back to Knightsbridge in the Ford Anglia – and the rodents were returned.

"What about hedgehog's testicles?"

"What about them?"

"They're a sixteenth century remedy for 'Pissying in the Bedde'."

"Rather you than me," said Mary Poppins.

Suzie got four A-levels, straight A's, and was offered places at Oxford, Bristol and Sussex.

Hector Dupuis, the celebrated Canadian M.P., returned his O.B.E., when the Beatles got theirs, protesting that the awards placed him on the same level as "vulgar nincompoops".

The Porge collected stamps in a desultory fashion, had sexual fantasies, involving Christine Keeler, developed dark circles under his eyes and barely muddled through. He seriously considered becoming a monk. The thought of going to bed with a girl and waking up in a puddle was simply too much to bear. Oh, the shame of it all.

Suzie went to Sussex, principally because her latest object of desire was a drummer who resided in Hove, where he seemed to spend all his considerable free time in the King Alfred Ten

Pin Bowling Lanes there – to the extent that his right arm was now two inches longer than his left.

Tom Foster-Wilson, having spent the last five years away at school in Canterbury, went to Sussex too. And Tom's friend, Anton, went up to Edinburgh, to read medicine.

The Porge's formal education came to a predictably damp and squibbish end. He did acquire one A-level – just. Then he left, in whatever the opposite is of a blaze of glory, and took the bus into town, where he mingled with the crowds that were gathering in Leicester Square for the premiere of the Vulgar Nincompoops' new film, "Help!".

That just about summed the whole thing up.

"Help!"

6

ZIMMERMAN PLUGS IN

When Tom Foster-Wilson was thirteen, his voice broke.

At Sussex, it broke down.

It was the drugs.

His speech decelerated to such an extent, that he gave up normal conversation as we know it, and in so far as he spoke at all, he tended to speak only in terms of whatever substance it was that happened to be re-arranging his brain-cells at that particular moment in time.

"Hi, Tom," you might say to him, "where were you last night?"

"Red Leb," he might drawl in the time it would take an average person to recite a sonnet.

Translation: "I spent the night at home in my room."

"Good morning, Tom. How are you?"

"Acapulco Gold."

Translation: "I'm extremely well, thank you."

"Tom, fancy a game of tennis?"

"Nepalese Temple Balls."

Translation: "You must be joking."

"Tom, what's so funny?"

"Durban Poison."

Translation: "Anything and everything."

"Tom, do you fancy coming out to eat?"

"Thai sticks."

Translation: "God, yes, I'm so hungry, I could eat an entire elephant vindaloo, with a baked rhinoceros or two on the side, and for pudding, at least a couple of tons of butterscotch flavoured Bird's Eye Instant Whip."

"Tom, what's the matter?"

"Home Grown."

Translation: "I don't think much of this dope."

"Tom, where did you park the Moke?"

"Kashmiri Twist."

Translation: "I can't remember."

Caroline and Hugo Foster-Wilson had divorced, in the wake of the latter's liaison with his dentist's receptionist. Hugo then upped sticks and decamped to Minneapolis of all places, minus the dental receptionist, to work in a counting house there. Caroline retreated to her parents in Devizes. Number Eleven was let to a Japanese diplomat and his family. But Tom, who could actually achieve surprising levels of fluency, when it suited him, persuaded her she had to have a pied-à-terre in town. So she bought the lease on a two-bedroom flat in the basement of a house in Thurloe Square, which, apart from his mother's occasional trips up to town, for shopping and doctors and lunch and the like, was Tom's exclusive domain. He had the Moke, the Mini Moke. Remember them? He had money, in the form of an injudiciously generous allowance. And, despite his mother's protests, he had not had a shave nor cut his hair in almost a year and three quarters. In short, Tom was having the time of his life.

Suzie ditched the drummer in favour of an extremely tall post-graduate student of antipodean extraction, whose idea of foreplay was to read The Lord of The Rings aloud to each other in bed.

When she mentioned this eccentricity to Tom, one giggly afternoon in May, he became so doubled up with mirth that he split the seat of his green crushed-velvet loons and, what with one thing and another, they ended up in bed.

Sexual relations, however, did not occur, because Tom forgot to stay awake – and Suzie suddenly remembered where she ought to have been, which was at a tutorial on Memory and Dreams. But that was the end of the extremely tall antipodean.

The following day, May 26, 1966, Tom and Suzie drove up to town in the Moke to see Bob Dylan at the Royal Albert Hall. Dylan had played the Manchester Free Hall on the seventeenth, and during the second half of that show, when Dylan was accompanied by The Hawks (later to become The Band) some folkie die-hard anti-electric acoustic conservative had shouted out: "Judas!" – to which the world's greatest living poet had replied: "I don't believe you", then turned to the boys in the band and snarled: "Play fucking loud!"

Word of Dylan's conversion to electricity and the Judas altercation had reached Tom's ears, and he was agog with excitement and indignation, and became momentarily verbal: "Fucking folkie wanker. Judas? Judas to whom? To himself? Jesus is Judas? Mind you, you can't have one without the other. Jesus without Judas is a whole different story, I mean ...... anyway ...."

Tom spent the morning happily baking: well, removing the tops off of Mr.Kipling's individual apple pies, stuffing them with his own patent mixture of two parts Afghani Black to one part Panama Red, replacing the tops, and popping them in the oven at Gas Mark 4 for seventeen minutes and thirty-two seconds.

He ate one before departure – and handed Suzie the tickets and the keys to the Moke.

He ate another one as they trudged up Exhibition Road from Thurloe Square, where they had parked the Moke outside the flat, heading for the Royal Albert Hall.

And he ate a third one during the interval.

In the second half, Dylan came on with the Hawks: Robbie Robertson (guitar); Richard Manuel (piano); Garth Hudson (organ); Rick Danko (bass, background vocals); Mickey Jones (drums).

"Mmmm," said Tom, retrieving a crumb, which was trapped in his shaggy moustache, "Mr.Kipling does make exceedingly good cakes." He closed his eyes.

Somewhere in the middle of "Just Like Tom Thumb's Blues", he slumped in his seat with a beatifically vacant expression on his face, finally overcome by an accumulation of Kiplings. He had gone to the moon, two days ahead of Gemini 9 – and he would not be back for some time.

Which was all very well for Tom, but what was Suzie supposed to do with him meanwhile?

She could not very well leave him there, a comatose heap in his seat at the Albert Hall. Or could she? She gave his tie-dye tummy a far from friendly prod. He grunted. Perhaps she would just leave him there. Serve him right.

At which point, Victor Blair stepped into the proceedings.

He had been watching. He had seen her annoyance and watched her prod Tom's tum. He'd seen her buttocks shift and lift beneath the far-from-opaque star-spangled fabric of her short short skirt. He had watched her leaning over to retrieve her matching, star-spangled, draw-string bag from somewhere underneath Tom's seat. He saw her golden hair fall forward on Tom's lap.

"Oh my God," thought Victor, "is that erotic, or what?"

"Ahem," said Victor.

Suzie looked up and saw him standing there, with his biceps and his t-shirt and his glasses and his short curly hair. If Marlon Brando had married Woody Allen, and they had had a son, it might well have turned out looking much like Victor Blair.

"Need any help?"

"He's crashed out," said Suzie, and stood up.

"So I see," said Victor, surprised to find himself looking **up** at her. She was taller by a head.

"Any suggestions?"

Victor flexed his knees, reached his well-manicured hands in under Tom's armpits, and hoisted him over his shoulder. He grinned at Suzie.

"I'm Victor, by the way."

"Suzie," said Suzie. "Follow me."

Victor followed – out of the row and up the aisle. He followed her star-spangled buttocks. He'd have followed those buttocks to hell and back, no matter how heavy the load.

In the foyer, he was accosted by an official, anxious to know whether medical assistance was required.

"No it's not," said Victor peremptorily. "This is Lord Porchester, and I am his butler. Get out of my way."

Suzie laughed and carried on.

Victor made it as far as the Royal Geographical Society, where he dropped his load in an unceremonious heap on the pavement of Kensington Gore, beneath the statue of David Livingstone there.

"Are you alright?"

"I'm fine. I'm fine," said Victor, and sat himself down beside Tom. "My God, I'm schwitzing here." He wiped his brow with a bicep. His glasses slipped down his nose. He took them off. He squinted up at her. A bus rumbled by.

"My God, you're a beautiful woman," he said.

Suzie had never been called a beautiful woman before. She had been called a beautiful girl – and a chick and a babe and a bird and a doll – but never a woman.

She smiled.

He groaned.

"Are you sure you're alright?"

"It's the physical exertion," said Victor. "It makes me so damn horny."

"Look," she said, "why don't I run on ahead and get the car?"

"A car would be good."

She laughed, kicked off her platforms, and sprinted off into the night.

Tom opened his eyes in a dormousey manner, looked about, said: "Far out", and drifted off again.

"You schmuck," said Victor.

Suzie ran all the way. A beautiful barefoot young woman, fit as a fiddle, racing through the night. Back down Exhibition Road. Past the Science Museum. past the Natural History Museum. Over Cromwell Road – and left into Thurloe Square.

She jumped into the Moke, inserted the key into the ignition, and turned it. She stepped on the gas.

Physical exertion made Suzie horny too.

Nine and a half weeks later, on the day that Lenny Bruce died, Victor and she were wed.

To celebrate the union, Chairman Mao Tse-Tung declared a Cultural Revolution.

7

"WHAT KEPT GODOT"

Victor was tremendously impressed when Suzie told him that her parents had always slept in separate rooms.

"That's cool," he said.

"Precisely," said she.

But then, of course, at Number Nine they had plenty of rooms to be separate in.

In their one-room apartment in Brighton, on the wrong side of the tracks, this kind of sophisticated arrangement was simply not on the cards. Cocooned as they were at that time, though, in a fever of newly married lust, propinquity was more blessing than curse, i.e. they couldn't keep their hands off each other.

Felix and Jennifer had always been able to keep their hands off each other. That was the way their lives had been arranged – by him. They undressed in separate rooms – she in her dressing-room, he in his bedroom, up one flight of stairs on the second floor landing.

If Felix wanted Jennifer, he went to her bedroom, and if the door was left ajar, he went in and closed the door behind him.

If Jennifer wanted Felix, she left her door ajar and hoped that Felix would come, padding along the corridor in his Tricker slippers and Turnbull and Asser pyjamas.

Jennifer never went to Felix's room. His door was never ajar.

Once, in **their** newly-married-lust phase, such as it was, she had left the door open and waited – in vain. So, she climbed the one flight of stairs and stood outside his room's closed door.

Surely, she thought, he must be able to hear the blood singing in me, feel my heat.

His bed-time reading that night? Singularly detumescent matter:

"Ten Nazi war criminals mounted the gallows erected in the prison gymnasium at Nurenberg early today. Two were missing: Hitler's deputy, Martin Bormann, believed dead, tried 'in absentia'; and Hermann Goering, who had committed suicide a few hours earlier with a cyanide pill."

Felix wondered how on earth the beastly cheat had been allowed to get away with that.

"There were three black-painted wooden scaffolds in the long, wide room. Two were used alternately, the third being kept in reserve.

"First to enter the execution chamber was Joachim von Ribbentrop, Foreign Minister in the regime that was to last a thousand years. The time was 1.11am. His arms were seized by two army sergeants as he walked through the door. Handcuffs were replaced by a leather strap. He climbed the 13 steps to the platform without hesitation, gave his name in a loud voice and, as the black hood was placed on his head, said 'I wish peace to the world.' The trap was sprung and he fell from view, hidden behind a dark curtain.

"Field Marshall Wilhelm Keitel, who had told the tribunal he had just obeyed orders, was next. His last words were: 'More than two million German soldiers went to their death for the Fatherland. I follow now my sons – all for Germany.'

"Ernst Kaltenbrunner, successor to Heydrich, the Butcher of Prague, licked his lips and glanced around him; Alfred Rosenberg, chief exponent of the master race theory, had nothing to say; Hans Frank, governor of Poland and a recent convert to Catholicism, came in smiling; Wilhelm Frick, 'Protector' of Bohemia, stumbled as he mounted the (13) steps; Julius

Streicher screamed 'Heil Hitler!' and could be heard groaning after he fell through the trap; Fritz Sauckel, the slave labour boss, limped on his left club foot up the (13) steps; General Alfred Jodl, in his Wehrmacht uniform, was haggard and nervous; last to die was Arthur Seyss-Inquart, Hitler's governor in Austria, who called for peace and understanding between peoples. Between executions, hangmen and guards were allowed to light up cigarettes."

When he heard his wife's hesitant knock at the door, Felix looked up over his half-moon specs and said:

"Come in."

She turned the cool knob, opened the door.

She swallowed. Her throat, her lips were dry, were parted.

"Is anything the matter?" enquired the armadillo, with genuine kindly concern.

"I thought you might .... want me."

"No, no, no, darling," said Felix, "don't you worry yourself about me. You run along to bed."

Was he being deliberately obtuse? She wished in a way that he was; but she knew that he was not.

"Felix?"

"What is it, my dear?"

"May I ask you a question?"

"Of course you may."

"Do you really love me?"

"Of course I do, my darling. What a question. Now, off to Bedfordshire with you and sleep tight."

"Good night, Felix."

"Good night, precious one," he said, simply unaware of anything amiss.

Jennifer withdrew.

When Felix died, Mary Poppins was moved out of her room on the top floor, down one flight of stairs, and into Felix's room.

The Porge, having learnt how to climb out of his cot, was moved into Suzie's bed in the nursery. And Suzie, on her return from hospital was moved into Mary Poppins' room.

Between them, Jennifer and Mary carried the cot down to the basement, where it was stored away, until such time, in the dim and distant future, as it might once again be needed.

The future turned out to be far less dim and distant than Jennifer would have liked.

In the way of things, Mary Poppins was the first to be told: that Suzie had married Victor Blair, without telling anybody, in a drab civil service in Brighton.

"Are you pregnant?"

"Certainly not."

"Well, that's a blessing."

"Mary, darling, you'll tell Mummy for me, won't you, please?"

"No, I won't."

"Petty, pretty please."

"You'll tell her yourself, my girl," said Mary, and there was no getting around her.

"Are you pregnant?" asked Jennifer, when Suzie spilled the beans.

"Why does everyone assume that because I get married I have to be pregnant?"

"Are you?"

"Were you pregnant when you married Daddy?"

"No."

"Well, neither am I."

"Well, good."

"What's good about it? Or bad about it? What difference would it make? The point is that I love Victor, and Victor loves me, and that's all you need to know. We're happy, for God's sake!"

"Well, I'm very pleased to hear it. And what do Victor's people think of all this?"

"Victor doesn't have people. He has parents."

Jennifer failed to grasp the distinction, but let the slight go by.

"Are his parents as happy as I ought to be that you and their son are so happy?"

"I have no idea," said Suzie. "I've never met them."

"Indeed?"

"Victor doesn't speak to them."

"Really? And why is that?"

"Because they fell out."

"I am not an idiot, Susan. If you want to speak to me woman to woman, then you have to credit me with some intelligence. Why did Victor fall out with his parents?"

The thought of speaking to her mother "woman to woman" was a new one on Suzie. It made her feel childlike and tearful inside, and she had to summon up all her strength to stop herself from blubbing.

"Because he changed his name."

"From?"

"Abrahams."

"Oh, I see. You mean, he's Jewish."

"What's wrong with that?"

"I'm sure I haven't any idea what's wrong with being Jewish. Perhaps you should ask Victor. After all, he's the one who changed his name from Abrahams to Blair."

Good point.

It all started when Victor decided that he was a writer and wrote his first novel – "What Kept Godot".

He wrote it in his spare time, when he wasn't working in his father's delicatessen in St. John's Wood.

In the story, Godot meets the narrator (Victor) in a coffee bar. Victor proceeds to explain to Godot *The Meaning of Life*. Godot is so spell-bound by Victor's existential expertise that he cannot bear to tear himself away and .... well, that's about it on the plot front.

On the readability front, "What Kept Godot" made Kant's "Critique of Pure Reason" read like "Murder on the Orient Express".

Needless to say, Victor thought he had written a masterpiece and sent it off to publishers as soon as the ink on the final exclamation mark was dry.

One poor man, at Macmillan, who actually read the whole thing, because he liked the title, wrote him a brief and lucid note: "Dear Mr Blair, I return herewith your so-called novel, 'What Kept Godot'. It is twaddle. Yours etcetera ......"

"Who is this Victor Blair?" Victor's father wanted to know, as the rejection slips, addressed to Victor Blair, started landing on the mat.

"I've written a book," said Victor. "I changed my name to Blair."

"Why would you do such a thing?"

"What kind of a question is that?" snapped Victor, moving into interrogative attack mode. "You don't ask writers why they write. They write."

"Why would you change your name?" Mr Abrahams persisted.

"Well, I changed my name **to** Blair as a kind of tribute to George Orwell, who changed his name **from** Blair."

"Why would you change your name, unless you were ashamed."

"I should be ashamed? Why should I be ashamed?"

"You tell me, Victor."

"Dad, did Tony Curtis get this grief because he changed his name from Bernie Schwartz? Jesus Christ!"

"You think that taking the name of another religion's God in vain is any the less offensive?"

"You like Jack Benny."

"So what?"

"He changed his name from Joseph Kubelsky, so what. Is Jack Benny ashamed?"

"Is he my son?"

"Dad, is this such a problem?"

"**I** am ashamed."

"Why should you be ashamed?"

"Why should I be ashamed? I shouldn't be ashamed that my son is ashamed that other people might think that he's Jewish? That's not shaming? That's not shameful?"

"It's not like that."

"No? What's it like then .... Mr Writer?"

Victor tried to over-ride the scorn in his father's voice.

"It's .... I .... you see, it's a question of perception. I don't want people to react to me as a **Jewish** writer. I want people to respond to my work on its own merits."

"So you're not Jewish?"

"I don't see myself as part of a Jewish literary tradition. No. I'm assimilated. I'm British."

"Victor," said Victor's father, with a voice that was dreadfully quiet, "you're Jewish – and don't you ever forget it."

"Listen, Dad, as far as I'm concerned, being Jewish is a problem in a pogrom, and that's about the beginning and the end of it."

"A problem in a pogrom? Is that what you think?"

"In a nutshell – yes."

There was a long long pause, during which the son regarded the father with cool defiance – and the father regarded the son with anger and dismay.

Abrahams knew from pogroms – first hand.

"You want to know what I think?"

"I'm sure you're going to tell me."

"You want to be a writer? You want to be judged on your merits? You have no merits, because you don't have the balls to face up to what you are, because you're not a man, you're not a mensch, because you're a shame on your family and you're a shame on your race – and you are no longer .... my son."

"What's that supposed to mean?"

"You want to be a Gentile? Go and be a Gentile some place else!"

Victor shivered and blinked. This **was** an existential moment. Reality's cold wind blew cobwebs from his brain. And in this moment, there was nothing between himself and **it**.

"And don't bother turning up to work," said his father. "You're fired. Now get out of my house."

The old man looked at his son, who was still his son, whether he liked it or not, just as Victor was still Jewish, whether he liked it or not. Then he turned, went up the stairs, went into his room, sat on his bed, put his head in his hands – and wept.

The Abrahams did not sleep in separate rooms – but they did sleep in separate beds.

Victor's mother, Audrey, sat bolt upright in hers. She did not have to ask her husband what had just occurred. She had heard. It was a small house, and the bedroom door had been open.

She looked at her husband, on the end of his bed, head in his hands. She watched his heaving back. This was by no means the first time that she had seen him cry. The Rings of Satan had sliced through their life more than their fair share of times.

She heard the front door slam, climbed out of bed, crossed to the window, peered out through the clean net curtains. She saw her son, with a sheaf of rejection slips in one hand and a manuscript in the other, striding off down Melrose Avenue – a street which in years to come would be rendered macabre by Nielsen, the boiler of men.

She sensed a spring in Victor's step, a jaunty spring, as, without so much as a glance back over his shoulder, he headed for Willesden Green and disappeared.

"He's not coming back," said Victor's mother – and sighed.

Victor's father rose and blew his nose.

"Good," he replied. "Good riddance."

8

SEX & SHOPPING

Victor found a room, a garret no less, in gloomy Camden Town.

An Italian delicatessen in nearby Primrose Hill was looking for staff. If you can slice smoked salmon, and Victor had been slicing smoked salmon since he was seven years old, you can certainly slice salami. He applied for the job, in the name of Blair, and was taken on. His salary? A joke, but it paid his rent, and as his father was wont to say: "You work in a food shop, you don't go hungry."

He changed his name by deed-poll and said goodbye to Abrahams for good. He acquired a set of weights from a bric-a-brac shop in Finsbury Park. "What Kept Godot" was stashed away in a shoe box in his cupboard in Camden Town.

Nothing daunted, Victor picked up his Osmiroid and began to pen "Sex & Shopping".

Well, ten out of ten for the title, which was sharp and snappy and years ahead of its time.

The trouble was, though, being Victor, it had precious little to do with either sex or shopping.

The plot was contained in the first and last sentence of each of its seventeen chapters –

First sentence of the first chapter: "Jack and Jill went to the shops to buy a loaf of bread."

Last sentence of the first chapter: "Then they went home and had sex."

First sentence of the second chapter: "Jack and Jill went to the shops to buy a needle and thread."

Last sentence: "Then they went home and had sex."

First sentence of the third chapter: "Jack and Jill went to the shops to buy a washing-up brush."

Last sentence: "Then they went home and had sex."

You get the picture.

There were some potentially intriguing off-page developments, in chapters seven, nine and thirteen.

First sentence of the seventh chapter: "Jack and Jill went to the shops and bought some margarine."

"Then they went home and had sex."

First sentence of the ninth chapter: "Jack and Jill went to the shops and bought some PVC."

"Then they went home and had sex."

Chapter thirteen began: "Jack and Jill went to the shops and bought a second-hand whip."

"Then they went home and had sex."

And the story seemed to come to a rather romantic conclusion, because at the beginning of chapter seventeen, the last chapter, "Jack and Jill went to the shops and bought a diamond ring."

"Then they went home and had sex."

Unfortunately, between these first and last sentences, there stretched interminable Himalayan ranges of absolutely impenetrable pseudo-philosophical gobbledygook, as Jack and Jill, on the way to whichever shop it was, to make whatever purchase it happened to be, discussed "The Meaning of Life". And then they went home and had sex.

Victor, himself, had sex on Sunday afternoons, with a hooker who lived in a basement flat on the fringes of Maida Vale. He had been given her number by a man he met at his cousin's bar mitzvah in 1952. "You should go and see Pearl," the man had said. "She'll sort you out." Victor was eighteen years old.

(In 1964, therefore, the year he left home, he was thirty! And, God knows, he had no intention of leaving, up to the moment his father slung him out. It was all so very convenient.)

And every Sunday afternoon thereafter, off he went, at a brisk trot.

His mother, who had been worrying plenty about Victor in that department, was overjoyed, convinced that at last he had found himself a girl.

"When are we going to meet her?"

"Meet who?"

"Do we know her?"

"She doesn't exist."

"Don't tell me she isn't Jewish."

"Mother, I'm going for a walk."

"In this weather?"

He missed these conversations with his mother, when he went. They were about the only things he did miss. The endless ways she tried to find out what he was up to, where, and with whom, every Sunday afternoon.

Victor's visits to Pearl suited him down to the ground. They were so convenient. He had the highest regard for her profession, which he found mysterious and strange, and probably existential.

And of course the great thing about prostitution is that prostitution is the place where sex and shopping meet. In prostitution, sex and shopping find their perfect expression – and fuse.

Otherwise, he was a monk. He walked to work, to Lorenzo's in Primrose Hill. He walked home, to his garret in Camden Town. He lifted his weights – and he wrote. On a couple of occasions, when he was totally stuck, he went to a movie.

Once, to see Issur Danielovitch Demsky's new film, "Seven Days in May", from which, had he paid attention, he might have learned a thing or two about plotting and suspense and all that. But he was far too busy wondering whether Issur Demsky would ever have got the part if he had not changed his name to Kirk Douglas.

More significantly, he went to see John Ford's "Cheyenne Autumn", a film of which the critic, Stanley Kauffman, wrote: "The acting is bad, the dialogue trite and predictable, the pace funereal, the structure fragmented and the climaxes puny."

Victor did not care. As far as he was concerned, any film which featured Emanuel Goldenberg in the cast, however small the part, was worth viewing.

"Sex & Shopping" took him more than two whole years to complete. And when it was (complete), he sent it off to publishers, who duly sent it back.

After the nineteenth rejection slip, including one on which someone had had the temerity to suggest that Victor should do something so banal as tell a story, he put "Sex & Shopping" in his cupboard in another shoe box, and wondered if he would ever write another line again.

It was his day off. The sun was shining. He went to the cinema. Another Emanuel Goldenberg classic. "The Cincinatti Kid". And once again the question that exercised Victor's brain was: Would Goldenberg have got the part, and all those other wonderful parts he played, without having changed his name to Edward G. Robinson?

He emerged, blinking, from the cinema. Now it was raining.

Victor walked – and walked – and walked.

From Camden Town to Tottenham Court Road. From Tottenham Court Road to Marble Arch. From Marble Arch, across Hyde Park, to the Albert Memorial. From the Albert Memorial, over Kensington Gore, to the Royal Albert Hall.

On a poster announcing forthcoming attractions, Bob Dylan's name caught his attention. Now here was another Jew, who had changed his name, and seemed to be doing OK. Perhaps it would be wise to check him out. Victor went inside and bought a ticket.

Then he went home and didn't have sex.

9

KETCHUP

Wake up. Get up. Strip bed. Have bath. Dress. Gather up sheets and put them in the washing-machine. Eat breakfast. Go to work. Work. Come home. Have supper. Watch television. Play Scrabble or Monopoly or Racing Demons with Mary Poppins. Lose, probably. Make bed. Undress. Brush teeth. Get into bed. Go to sleep.

Life, for the Porge, was nothing if not dull.

No sex. No drugs. No rock and roll. No Afghan coats nor green crushed velvet loons. No joss sticks. No patchouli. No denim.

For work, two staid grey suits from the Army and Navy Stores summer sale, one not quite so dark as the other, and five white shirts from Marks and Spencer. For the weekend, Viyella checks, one double-breasted blazer with flat brass buttons, one brown Harris tweed jacket, and two pairs of Cavalry twill trousers.

He worked as a junior teller at the Oxford Circus branch of Barclays Bank. He did not mind the work. It was mindless. He did not mind his life. His life was mindless too. If someone had given him a gun and told him to stick it in his mouth and pull the trigger, he would not have minded that either. He really didn't care.

Sometimes, in his lunch break, he would walk to Carnaby Street. Up one side went the Porge, and down the other, with a puzzled Prince-Charles-at-an-Acid-House-Party look on his face – then went back to work again. Time Magazine had recently declared: "In this century, every decade has its city .... and for the Sixties that city is London."

And for Swinging London, the decade's street was Carnaby Street. Unprepossessing, run-down, dingy little Carnaby Street – no more! This was where it was happening, man. The hub. The happy hub. The turned-on, tuned-in, super-cool, psychedelic, optimistic FAR OUT HUB! It was not at the centre, though, of any universe the Porge could even recognise, let alone inhabit. He could not get to grips with it at all, at all. He was a stranger in a strange land. No map. No phrase book. No rule book. Not a tourist. He did not smile. He was, in fact, an alien altogether. He was in the wrong dimension, in the wrong galaxy, in the wrong body, in the hopelessly wrong frame of mind.

"Whatever are we going to do with him, Mary?" Jennifer Perry would wonder. "He's so …….. meek."

"Then he'll probably inherit the earth," said Mary. "Leave him alone. He'll be fine."

"Can't you talk to your brother?" his mother persisted to Suzie, one afternoon over tea in the Fountain Room at Fortnum's.

"He doesn't talk my language, ma," said Suzie, who was tucking into a knickerbocker glory that was giving her kaftan a run for its money in the technicolour stakes.

"What nonsense," said Jennifer. "You can both talk decent plain English."

"Mummy, I didn't come all this way up town to talk about the Porge."

"You shouldn't call him the Porge."

"Why not? He is the Porge."

"He doesn't like it."

"He loves it."

"No, he doesn't."

"Mummy."

"Yes, darling."

"I'm pregnant."

"I see."

"What's that supposed to mean?"

"You told me you weren't."

"I wasn't .... then. I am .... now."

"Well, what can I say?"

"How about 'Congratulations'?"

Jennifer did congratulate her daughter, then proceeded to lay down the law about the impossibility of bringing up a child in a one-room hovel in Brighton without any visible means of support.

"It's not a hovel, and I've got my grant – and Victor's got a job."

"What kind of a job?"

"He's working in a deli in the Lanes."

"Earning how much?"

"None of your business!"

"How much?"

"Twelve pounds a week."

"Pathetic."

Jennifer said that under the circumstances, there was only one sensible practical course of action to pursue. Victor and Suzie would have to leave Brighton and come back to Number Nine to live. They could have the top floor.

"What about my degree?"

"I haven't got a degree," said Jennifer, with a degree of illogicality. "Perhaps, if you hadn't gone off to university in the first place, you wouldn't have got yourself into this mess."

"It's not a mess."

"Yes, it is. Apart from which, what with one extra-curricular activity and another, I can't imagine the chances of your actually getting a degree to be particularly high. No, there's nothing for it, you'll have to come home and have your baby. At least you'll be warm and safe."

Suzie picked up her maraschino cherry, from the saucer where she had been saving it till last (like father like daughter) and popped it into her mouth. She licked her luscious lips and laughed.

"What's so funny?" Jennifer wanted to know.

"I can't tell you how much I was hoping that that was what you were going to say," she confessed – and grinned.

"Well, where am I supposed to sleep?" demanded the Porge, when he heard the news, that evening, in the kitchen.

"You can move into the study," said Jennifer.

"I don't want to move into the study. I like my room."

"You've slept in that room all your life."

"So?"

"A change will do you good."

Mary Poppins removed the shepherd's pie from the oven, and placed it on the mat in the centre of the table, where it steamed between the mother and the son.

"I don't want to move into the study."

"Why not? There's a lot less stairs to climb." (The study was on the first-floor half landing.) "It's a lovely room. Your father loved that room. He said it was the best room in the house."

Mary Poppins strained the peas, tipped them from the colander into a bowl, popped a knob of butter on top and placed them on the table.

"If it's such a great room, why don't **you** move into it then? Victor and Suzie can have your room."

"No they can't, George."

"Why not?"

Jennifer considered her response.

Mary Poppins seized the serving-spoon, dug into the shepherd's pie, removed a Porge-sized portion with a squelch and deposited it on his plate.

"I said – Why not?"

"I'm not as young as I used to be," Mary intervened. "I wouldn't mind not having so many stairs to climb. Why don't I move down to the study, and the Porge can have my room? Help yourself to peas."

"Well," said Jennifer, "what do you say to that?"

The Porge did not say anything to that. He glared at his plate. A vein throbbed at his temple. What he said was:

"Where's the ketchup!"

"In case you don't remember, Porge," said Mary, fixing the rude young man with a steely eye, "you finished up all the ketchup on your fish fingers last night."

"Well, why the hell didn't you get some more! How am I supposed to eat bloody shepherd's pie without ketchup! It's impossible!"

"George ...." Jennifer began.

"Oh, leave me alone!"

Barely containing his tears, he threw back his chair, so it crashed over to the red and black checkerboard linoleum floor, stomped over to the door, slammed it behind him, and ran up the four flights of stairs to his room.

(First flight to the first half-landing and the study. Second flight to Jennifer's bedroom and dressing-room. Third flight to the second half-landing and Mary Poppins' room, Felix Perry's bedroom as was. Fourth flight to the top floor ....)

Away above them, Jennifer and Mary heard the door of the nursery slam. They clearly imagined him throwing himself face downward on the bed.

In unison, the two women sighed.

Mary went to pick up the chair.

"You know, Mary," said Jennifer, "I really don't think you should call him the Porge any more."

"I don't see why I shouldn't," said Mary, "when he behaves like one."

10

THE STUDY

From Abrahams to Blair was a laughably tiddly step, when you consider that in July of 1917, the entire royal family changed its name from marvellous Saxe-Coburg-Gotha to boring Windsor, in a bid to bamboozle their subjects into thinking that they weren't Saxe-Coburg-Gothas at all, but ever so frightfully English. It was an old trick, but it might just work. It had to work. These were desperate times. In March, the Czar had lost his throne. The Czar was the King's first cousin. A year later he had been murdered in a basement. The shit was truly hitting the fan – right, left and centre.

Of course, it was not until the royal wedding of 1981, when the Windsors, in the body of Prince Charles, conjoined with the Spencers, in the body of Lady Diana, that the Saxe-Coburg-Gothas could have been said truly to have arrived in the English upper classes.

For Victor, marrying Susan Perry, and moving into Number Nine, represented much the same kind of achievement.

And from the very first day he arrived at Number Nine, when Suzie gave him the guided tour, Victor had his eye on the study.

"Hey. Nice room."

Now here was a room in which a man could write a Pulitzer-prize-winning work. It was not large, about thirteen by thirteen feet, but its elements contrived, in Victor's eyes, to make it perfect: the curved casement window, with its window-seat in faded chintz, which overlooked the garden; the cream-painted panelling; the built-in bookshelves; and the portrait of Susan's great-grandfather, Brigadier Perry, over the fireplace. Into this fireplace, in days gone by, Felix would knock out his pipe of an evening before retiring. Then he would climb the second flight of stairs, pause a moment outside Jennifer's room, and wonder, if the door was open, whether or not to go in.

When Victor arrived at Number Nine, however, the study was spoiled by the recently installed presence of the Porge's single bed.

In the event, Mary Poppins had remained where she was in her room on the second half-landing. The argument about her legs, and not getting any younger, worked both ways. Had she moved into the study, she would certainly have been nearer the ground, but, come the birth of the imminent infant, she would have been two flights further away from the nursery, where her presence was bound to be needed. So she stayed put.

And on mature reflection, when he came to think about it, it dawned upon the Porge that, in the event of strangers in the house, the study was nearer to the washing-machine by far. Under the circumstances, the downward move from the top of the house had this most practical pro, which outweighed all the other intangible cons: in the morning, he could strip his bed and whip the offending sheets down to the laundry in the basement, without much fear of being overseen.

The Porge did not know what to make of Victor. Therefore, he ignored him – pretended, in fact, that Victor did not exist.

If Victor came into the room, where the Porge was reading the Evening Standard, say, the Porge would pointedly not look up.

But should Victor have the gall to attempt communication, to start a conversation with his awkward young brother-in-law, the Porge would yawn, stretch, fold his paper, stand up and leave the room, without so much as a word.

Victor was nothing daunted. Come what may, down he came to breakfast in the morning, and, invariably, there the Porge would be, tucking into his Sugar Puffs, with half a banana cut up on top.

"Morning, George," said Victor, cheerful as could be.

The Porge did not respond.

And of an evening, there they would all be, sitting round the table in the kitchen, having supper, and Victor would try again.

"So, George, good day at the bank?"

But the Porge would not reply.

And if anyone tried to remonstrate with him on Victor's behalf, he would say something like:

"Excuse me a minute, I just have to ...."

Then, trailing off, he would push back his chair, leave the room and fail to return.

Jennifer, Mary and Susan were all variously angry with the Porge and apologetic on his behalf.

"Oh, I don't mind," said Victor. "It's funny. He's eccentric. He's a kid."

"He's not eccentric," said Jennifer. "He's rude."

"He's not a kid," said Mary Poppins. "He's old enough to know better."

Suzie wondered to Victor, alone in their room at the top of the house, if the reason for the Porge's anti-social behaviour might be Freudian.

"How come?""

"Well, you **are** fucking his sister."

"Hmmm," said Victor, with a leer, "that's an excellent idea." And he grabbed her, which put an end to that conversation.

Victor really was totally undiscombobulated by the Porge's refusal to recognise his existence. On the one hand, "as a writer", he found it interesting. It amused him. And, on the other hand, he was canny enough to recognise the fact that his treatment by the Porge was actually helping to consolidate his position in the household.

Most preposterous of all was the Porge's performance of a morning at the bus-stop.

On his return to London, Victor had presented himself, pretending that he just happened to be passing, at Lorenzo's in Primrose Hill, with a view to wondering whether, if by any chance ....

Victor did not even have to ask. Lorenzo was overjoyed to have him back.

"Iva binna practic'ly avvinanartattac, trying to finda someone who canna cutta the prosciutto lika you, Vittorio, my friend, my man, my son!"

Victor had no ego whatsoever about working in a delicatessen again, while at the same time being a great unpublished author. Or, rather, his ego was so enormous, and his opinion of whatever he happened to be doing at any one time was so high, that the effect was the same.

Besides, Victor liked Lorenzo's, and he needed some money, and the work was suitably mentally untaxing to keep his mighty brain free for contemplation of his forthcoming glorious contribution to the wonderful world of letters.

It was a hell of a trek from Barnes to Primrose Hill and back each day, involving a bus and a tube and a serious walk. Victor loved it though. Commuting, he claimed, cranked up his creative juices. He turned down lifts when he was offered them.

The route to Primrose Hill and the route to Barclays Bank in Oxford Circus shared a point of departure: the bus stop up the road from Number Nine.

So it was that Victor found himself leaving the house at the same time as the Porge, standing in the same bus queue as the

Porge, and climbing onto the same bus. And did the Porge acknowledge his presence? No, he did not.

Victor was ahead of the Porge in the queue. He turned about and grinned at his brother-in-law. The Porge looked straight through him.

The bus arrived. Victor got on, found himself an empty seat. He watched as the Porge cast about for a vacant space. There was only one – next to Victor, so the Porge elected to stand.

Up Castelnau trundled the bus. Over Hammersmith Bridge – and stopped at their mutual stop. The brothers-in-law alit. The Porge strode off, heading for the Piccadilly Line. Victor watched him go, bemused, amused and really quite astonished, even impressed. Then he strolled over to catch his train on the Metropolitan Line.

Three weeks of this and Victor decided to beard the Porge in his den.

He knocked on the door of the study. It was ten o'clock at night. Needless to say there was no reply, which is not to say that the Porge had X-ray vision and could see through the door. He knew, though, that whoever it was would only be coming to hassle him.

Victor turned the knob, opened the door, and entered.

The Porge was sitting on the window-seat, polishing his shoes. Cherry Blossom Black. Stiff Brush. Bright yellow duster.

"Hi," said Victor. "Hope you don't mind my barging in like this. There's just a couple of points I'd like to make."

The Porge gave him a furious get-the-fuck-out-of-here look, then returned his attention to his toe-caps, which he attacked with his brush with homicidal vigour.

"Mind if I sit down?"

The question was rhetorical. Victor parked himself on the edge of the bed.

Out of the corner of his eye, the Porge noticed that a tiny triangle of blue plastic undersheet had not been properly tucked in. Incorrectly convinced that Victor could see it, the poor boy died inside. It seemed to him as wide as the wide Sargasso Sea.

"Hey," said Victor, "I know what it's like. The longer you keep from speaking to someone, the more difficult it becomes to speak to them, to break the silence. I know what it's like. I've done it myself, when I was eight."

Brush-brush-brush-brush-brush-brush-brush.

Victor cast his eyes around the study. Never mind the Pulitzer. This was a no-question, no-doubt-about-it Nobel-prize-winning novel-writing room.

"You know what, George?" said Victor. "You know what you remind me of? You remind me of a story I once wrote. You know what it was called? The Butterfly."

Brush-brush-brush-brush-brush-brush-brush.

It was rubbish, of course. A lie. Victor had never written a story called The Butterfly. Not his kind of title at all.

"I'll tell you what it was about. It was about this caterpillar, see? A really miserable, grey, boring caterpillar, who spent his whole time crawling about at home and doing absolutely nothing at all with his life. But, you know what, somewhere, deep down inside himself, this caterpillar knew that somehow or other he had it in himself to be a really beautiful butterfly."

This really was not Victor's kind of story. Too cute by half. He knew absolutely nothing about caterpillars or butterflies. But he ploughed on, regardless.

The Porge picked up his bright yellow duster and set to polishing for all he was worth.

Rub-adub-adub-adub-adub-adub.

"Then, you know what happened next? There was this whole great concatenation of circumstances – I won't bore you with the details – but as a result of which, this miserable fucker of a caterpillar had to leave his home. He had to pack up his bags and go. But you know what? Zap! Next thing he knows, the caterpillar's sprouting wings, all over the fucking shop – and he's gone from boring grey to technicolour in a flash, and he's flying about, hither and thither, and, basically, having the time of his life."

Rub-adub-adub-adub-adub-adub.

By now, the Porge could see his pitiful face in the shine of his shoes.

"Well, end of bedtime story, George. I hope you got the point."

Rub-adub-adub-adub-adub-adub.

"The point is, Georgie boy, you've been tied to your Mummy's apron strings for far too long. Be a man. Be a mensch. You're too old to have a nanny. You're too old for Mary Poppins. You're too old to be a Porge. Pack your bags. Leave home. Fuck off."

Coming from Victor, as Victor was well aware, this was a bit rich. On the other hand, Victor had not been a misery at home. He had been busy-busy-busy, hadn't he, what with "What Kept Godot" and his trips to Maida Vale. He had had an agenda.

"Hey man," said Victor, "I've said enough. Good night. Sleep tight. Think about it."

Well, when Victor went, the Porge put down his duster, stood up, crossed the room, lay down on his bed and stared at the ceiling.

Astonishingly, this astonishing idea had never even crossed his mind before.

Leave home.

Now, what were the pros and cons of that?

11

PASTURES NEW

The Porge moved into Ifield Road on Sunday, July the Sixteenth.

Suzie had gone off with Tom to take part in the "Legalise Pot 1967" rally in Hyde Park.

Tom picked her up in the Moke. He patted Susie's pregnant tum and said: "Far out."

Victor considered punching him on the nose.

Suzie said: "You should come too, babe. It's important."

"Why's it important?" Victor wanted to know.

"Because, man," said Tom, lurching onto his one and only soap box, "whatever a man wants to do in the privacy of his own bloodstream shouldn't be anybody else's fucking business but his own."

In the way that Hercules Poirot did not "approve" of murder, Victor did not "approve" of drugs. He did not "approve" of anything which came between his genius and **it**. And he certainly did not "approve" of Tom.

"I've got more important fish to fry," said Victor.

Tom and Suzie disappeared off in the direction of Hammersmith Bridge.

Victor went into the conservatory, picked up the Perry family Bible, which he had commandeered for purposes of research, and perused it, listening out with half an ear for the Porge, who he knew was upstairs in the study.

He turned the pages of The Greatest Story Ever Told in a desultory fashion.

"Suppose ye that I am come to give peace on earth?" he read. "I tell you, Nay; but rather division: ……. The father shall be divided against the son, and the son against the father."

"Huh," said Victor to himself, "tell me about it."

A couple of pages further on, he came to the prodigal son, and the prodigal son's brother is complaining to the prodigal son's father, saying what a good boy he has always been: "But as soon as this thy son was come, which hath devoured thy living with harlots, thou hast killed for him the fatted calf."

"Harlots" leapt off the page.

It was Sunday. It was Sunday afternoon. If Victor and Suzie had never met, if Robert Zimmerman had not changed his name, he would have surely been with Pearl by now, banging his brains out for cash. It wasn't the sex (he told himself). It was the sharpness, the nearness to **it**. He could get to Maida Vale and be back in time for tea. Who would be any the wiser?

Old habits die hard. Victor laid the Good Book down and headed for the door.

As he approached it, the doorbell rang.

Now who could that be?

Victor opened the door.

"Cab for Mr Perry," said a man on the mat outside.

For a moment there, Victor failed to grasp who Mr Perry was.

"That's me," shouted the Porge, from the top of the first flight of stairs. "I'll be right down."

Moments later, the Porge appeared, dragging a heavy suitcase which he bump-bump-bumped down the stairs.

"You want a hand with that, George?"

The Porge ignored him, left the suitcase at the bottom of the stairs, ran back up the stairs and re-appeared with a cardboard Cream Cracker box, which he hefted down the stairs, past Victor in the hall, and out to the waiting taxi on the drive.

"What the hell," thought Victor.

He flexed his pecs, activated a bicep, lifted the suitcase with ease, carried it out to the cab and stashed it in the back.

"Well, well, well," said Victor.

The Porge pushed past him, went back into the house, then re-emerged with two bulging Army and Navy Store carrier bags.

"So, George? This is it? You're off?"

The Porge got into the cab and slammed the door.

Victor opened it and grinned at the Porge.

"You know what, George? You're an arsehole. But good luck anyway."

The Porge glared at him, grabbed the door-handle, then slammed the door shut again.

"Where to?" asked the cabbie.

Victor saw the Porge lean forward and mutter an address.

"Eh?" The cabbie couldn't hear.

The Porge leaned further forward and muttered once again.

"Oh, Ifield Road," proclaimed the cabbie, letting the cat out of the bag, via his open window. "Right. Got it."

And – exit the would-be lepidopterous Porge in a shiny black cab.

Jennifer Perry and Mary Poppins were on holiday, together, in Devon.

The year before last, The Mousetrap had celebrated its 5,000th performance, and in 1966 at the august August meeting of the Devon and Exeter Steeplechases and Hurdle Races, the "Mousetrap" Challenge Cup Handicap Steeple Chase was inaugurated, with a prize of £350, and Agatha Christie herself presenting the cup. This important literary/sporting event was to be the highlight of the Perry/Poppins trip, with the promise of a flutter, and possibly even the chance of glimpsing the Queen of Crime in the flesh.

In the wake of the Porge's departure for pastures new, the brothel-bound Victor cancelled his planned departure for pastures old. He had the house to himself.

He had the house to himself.

He savoured it.

He had been far too little on his own of late. The study beckoned. Pearl could wait.

Stripped, the Porge's bed was even more of an eyesore in the study than before. It was with Victor and his biceps, however, the work of an instant to manhandle the offending divan out of the door, down the stairs, onto the street and into the skip in front of Number Eleven.

The Japanese diplomat and his family having decamped, and the decree nisi having become absolute, Tom's mother, Caroline Foster-Wilson, had promptly and without further ado put the house up for sale. Shortly after Christmas, it was sold – to a property developer, whose plan it was to turn the house into flats. The work had only just begun. This being Sunday, no-one was about.

Victor had no qualms about disposing of so large a piece of the Perry's household furniture as a bed. This one was well past its use-by date.

"Well, I wouldn't sleep in it – and nobody can call me squeamish." That was Victor's line.

In a corner of the study was a roll-top desk.

Victor rolled up the roll-top.

It made a particularly gratifying sound.

There was paper in a packet in a bag on the nursery floor. Victor went to fetch it.

His pen was in the pocket of his jacket, which was hanging on the bedroom door.

White rectangle of paper, floating on a sea of seasoned oak.

Victor unscrewed his Osmiroid.

That laughable, bourgeois, reactionary, anally-retentive suggestion, the one that had the small-minded gall to imply that "telling a story" might be a good idea, had of late been beginning to bother Victor more than somewhat. Hence his recent research into this so-called Greatest Story Ever Told. He had even been to see the movie, featuring Marion Michael Morrison as the centurion. But now the time for research was over. He had studied the competition – Matthew, Mark, Luke and John. He had the longed-for study to himself. This was it. **It**! In the end, one way or another, it always comes down to this – you have to lay down some ink.

"Alright," said Victor. "You want the greatest story ever told? I'll give you the fucking greatest story ever told."

Victor aimed his Osmiroid at the empty page and wrote:

"In the beginning was the Word ...."

Yes. Alright. OK. So far, so good. A journey of a thousand miles begins with a single step. A masterpiece begins with a single Word.

"...... and the Word was God."

Yes, but, when he came to think about it, and he did come to think about it, there and then, with a vengeance – where did .....? I mean, what exactly .....? I mean, how could ......? I mean, you can't just .... or can you?

Victor hummed and Victor hawed. He stared into space for an aeon or two. And then it struck him. **It** struck him. Yes! He smiled. Oh, boy. Talk about negative capability.

Victor changed his full-stop into a comma and wrote:

", but before that there was **it**!"

So: "In the beginning was the Word, and the Word was God, but before that there was **it**!"

Oh-boy-oh-boy-oh-boy-oh-boy-oh-boy. Thank you, my muse. Oh, thank you.

A jubilant Victor proceeded to write a thousand words of

incomprehensible drivel, on the general topic of **it**, which he then read through – and tore up. Even Victor thought it was drivel. He placed the torn-up pieces of paper in the fireplace, under the eagle eye of Brigadier Perry. He struck a match – and, with pleasure, watched the merry flames, leaping in the grate.

"Oh boy," said Victor, "I love this room."

If only the Porge could have felt the same way about his new abode in Ifield Road.

The Baby Belling. The insignificant fridge. The threadbare carpet. The limp and unlined curtains in a nasty shade of green. The table with the torn blue-check Fablon top. The two sad chairs. The army surplus wardrobe. The asthmatic Ascot over the lime-stained sink. The dripping tap. The dismal communal bathroom down the hall. And, oh so lonely, in one corner, the bed.

The Porge sat down on the meagre swirly brown and orange mattress, in the middle of it, and each of the ends bent upwards, describing a curve in the shape of a humourless smile. This was the only trace of a smile in the room. The Porge's mouth described a curve, the ends of which bent downwards in distress.

From down below, the Porge could hear the sound of washing-machines and tumble-dryers. They were the reason why he'd chosen this particular address. His room was located over a laundromat.

The Porge stood up, with a hopeless sigh, and started to pull his specialised bedding out of the Cream Cracker box.

He made the bed.

First, his blue waterproof undersheet. Then his fitted drip-dry polyester bottom sheet. Then the top sheet. Two grey blankets came with the room. He tucked them in. Nice neat hospital corners, just as he had been taught by Mary Poppins. Last of all, the pillow. Having inserted it into his pillow-case, he tried to plump it up. Its plumping days were long gone by. No support there.

The Porge located his alarm clock in one of the Army and Navy Store bags, set it for the morning, undressed and climbed, with heavy heart, into the sad little bed.

As night fell, the neon of the laundromat below asserted itself in the street.

Strange and threatening shadows danced on the ceiling over his head.

The Porge had never been into a public laundering place. The prospect, on the morrow, filled him with dread.

He fell asleep, at last, to the sound of the distant sloshing machines.

He fell asleep – and slept the sleep of the dead.

He slept right through the alarm clock's strident ringing.

He slept right through to half past nine and woke, at last, to the sound of sinister singing: "Puppet on A String", badly out of tune. It was Saddam, the kitchen porter, from Swann's, the restaurant over the road, who was washing down the pavement with a mop.

The sun shone in through the grim green curtain, painting the room with menacing hues.

The Porge awoke and new at once that something was amiss.

"Half past nine! Oh my God!"

He would never get to work on time. He was centuries late already.

"Oh shit," he grumbled in desperation, and scrambled out of bed.

"Oh shit!" he exclaimed, in an altogether different tone of voice, when all of a sudden it dawned on him, what had just occurred, or, rather, what had not occurred.

An incredulous Porge approached the bed and pulled back the sheets.

"Oh shit!!"

They were dry.

He felt them.

Yes, they were dry.

He felt himself.

He was dry. He was clean.

The sun shone in through the jolly green curtain, painting the room in benevolent hues.

Saddam was singing – "Puppet on A String" – and it sounded pretty good. The tap was dripping in time. The washing machines sloshed along merrily below.

"Oh boy," said the Porge, "I love this room."

He danced about a bit with nothing on. Then he got dressed, went out, found a phone box and called the bank.

"Where are you, Perry? You're late," said Hickmott, a man with a permanent cold. "Are you sick?"

"Yes, I am."

"What's the matter with you?"

"I'm sick of counting other people's money."

"Pardon?" Hickmott sniffed.

"I'm sick of being bored beyond belief."

"Now look here."

"And you know what, Mr Hickmott, sir, I'm sick to death of you."

"You're what!"

"I'm sick to death of you – and your disgusting nasal drip."

"You're fired." Sniff. "Do you hear that, Perry?" Sniff. "D'you hear?"

"Receiving you loud and clear, Mr Hickmott. Receiving you loud and clear."

The Porge hung up on Hickmott then and there.

Oh, frabjous day! Callooh! Callay!

He beamed from ear to ear.

12

IT!

Victor was hoping **it** would be a girl, because Suzie disapproved of circumcision.

"So you don't like my penis?"

"I love your penis."

"But you wish it had a foreskin."

"Victor, I don't love you because your penis has or has not got a foreskin. I love you because, for some bizarre reason, I love you."

"But you wish I wasn't circumcised?"

"I didn't say that."

"You implied it."

"No, I didn't. Don't be so paranoid. All I said was that if the baby's a boy, I'm not having him circumcised."

"That doesn't imply criticism of my penis?"

"My criticism of circumcision is not a criticism of you. Surely, you must be able to see that."

"I see what I see."

"Don't give me that shit, Victor. Mutilating a defenceless baby's barbaric – and that's the beginning and the end of it."

"That's anti-semitic."

"No, it's not."

"Jews are barbaric? That's not anti-semitic?"

"That's syllogistic crap, and you know it. I never said Jews are barbaric. I said circumcision's barbaric."

"Q.E.D."

"Oh for God's sake, if I was anti-semitic, would I be married to you? How dare you call me anti-semitic!"

"Now who's being paranoid?"

"I am not paranoid, and I am not anti-semitic."

"I didn't say you were anti-semitic. I said, what you said was anti-semitic."

"Listen, Victor, if new-born babies could talk, do you honestly believe for one minute that they'd be in favour of having their foreskins chopped off."

"If they could talk, you'd be able to explain to them why it's a good idea."

"Oh yeah? Convince me."

"Well, it's cleaner .... for one thing. I mean, it's, er, more hygienic, isn't it?"

"Bullshit."

"Oh yeah? Smegma is bullshit?"

"What do you know about smegma?"

"Practically nothing at all, thank God."

"Personally, I think it's offensive for you to suggest that anyone who isn't circumcised is dirty."

"I didn't say that."

"I think it's anti-non-semitic."

"Christ, Suzie, can't you understand? I don't want my son to have a dick that's different from mine!"

"Aha!" said Suzie. "And thereby hangs a tale."

"Huh!" snorted Victor. "A man who could make so vile a pun would not scruple to pick a pocket."

"What pun? Oh." She laughed. She chuckled. "No pun intended. Honestly."

She chuckled some more. Her chuckle was infectious. Victor chuckled too.

"Anyway," said Victor, "it's going to be a girl."

"Called Daisy."

Victor sniffed: "Daisy's not bad, I suppose, if you happen to be a cow."

"Or Polly."

"If you give birth to a parrot, we'll call it Polly."

"If I give birth to a parrot, I'll blame it all on you and your circumcised cockatoo."

"Very witty. How about Phoebe?"

"I hate Phoebe."

"How can you hate Phoebe? It's a brilliant name. Literally. Phoebe. The shining one. I love Phoebe."

"I'm not having a daughter called Phoebe."

And she didn't.

But she did have a daughter, in Queen Charlotte's, at three thirty-six p.m., on Saturday the sixteenth of March, 1968, weighing in at six pounds and thirteen ounces, with all her bits in place.

"Holy shit," said Victor, wiping the tears from his eyes, "was that ever fucking cathartic or what!"

"Thanks for being with me," said Suzie, blitzed after fourteen and three-quarter hours of labour.

"I wouldn't have missed it for the world."

"I would." She was groggy.

"I think we're going to have to call her Bridget."

"Why?" She was foggy.

"Because, don't you see, she's a bridge between us and **it**. Bridget."

"What?" She gave a mighty yawn.

"Bridge – **it**. She's a bridge to **it**. Bridget."

"Huh" She yawned again. "What's **it**?" She closed her eyes.

"**It**! Come on, Suzie, you know. **It**. **It**'s the **it** that's in reality – re-al-**it**-y."

"Oh, fuck that," said Suzie and gave herself up to irresistible sleep with a deep and smiley sigh.

"You're something else," said Victor to his sleeping wife, stroked a lock of hair back off her forehead, kissed the baby gingerly, and left. There would be time enough tomorrow to continue with the name campaign. In the meantime, there was the cot to bring up from the basement, to clean, to repaint, to reinstate in the nursery where it belonged.

Jennifer and Mary Poppins came to see the baby the following day – in the morning.

"Isn't she beautiful?" said the proud mother of one.

"She looks just like Victor," said Jennifer, and failed to refrain from adding: "Poor little thing."

"She is beautiful," said Mary Poppins. "May I hold her?"

Suzie passed the infant parcel.

Mary Poppins held the child and cooed, lost for a moment in her own lost dreams.

"What would you call her, Mary, if she was yours?" asked Suzie, unaware that this question was cruel.

"Agatha," Mary replied, without a moment's thought.

And then she said, in a matter-of-fact, unmaudlin way, but choosing her words with care:

"Had Martin lived and ...... if we had ever had ...... the good fortune ...... to have had a little daughter of our own ...... I'd have called her Agatha." Then briskly. "But it wasn't to be, was it, little sausage?" And she gave the baby an Eskimo kiss.

"Has Victor told his parents?" Jennifer wanted to know, by way, more than anything else, of changing the subject.

Suzie said: "I doubt it."

"Don't you think he should?"

"That's up to him."

Victor popped in in the afternoon. It was Sunday afternoon.

"So? Bridget?"

"Not a chance. She doesn't look anything like a Bridget."

"She looks like a Bridget to me. Apart from which, if we call her Bridget, then that's what this particular Bridget will look like."

"How about Agatha?"
"Do me a favour."
"My mother thinks you should tell your parents."
"Oh does she?"
"Don't you think you should?"
"No, I don't. Do you?"
"Well, I think you'd be well pissed off if your daughter had a baby and didn't bother telling you about it."
"If I'd thrown her out of the house, for nothing, wouldn't it serve me right?"
"You're a hard man, Victor."
"Yeah. Maybe I am," said he, not unpleased at being so described.
Tom turned up: soft – stoned – fuzzy. Floppy hat. Mirrored shades. **Legalise It** t-shirt.
"What's it called?" he wondered, raising his shades to peer into the crib. It was hard to say which of the two, Tom or the baby, was more unfocussed.
"We can't decide," said Suzie.
"How about …….. Lennon?" Tom suggested.
"Tom, she's a girl," Suzie pointed out.
"So what?"
Suzie laughed.
"How about that, Victor? Lennon Blair?"
Victor, the hard man, glared and said he had to go – and went.
Sunday afternoon.
Victor hit the sidewalk, turned right out of the hospital, round the bend and heading for Shepherd's Bush, anywhere but home.
Pounding along, the lupanar's lure became increasingly strong.
"Hell," he thought, "this is all wrong. All wrong."
He increased his pace, determined to outwalk the lubricious thoughts which infiltrated his blood. But the faster he went,

and the further he went, the hornier he became. Park by park – Holland, Hyde and Green – his libido rose and rose, until, by the time he found himself marching past Buckingham Palace, he determined that, to hell with it, he owed himself a trip to Maida Vale. He was a new father, for goodness' sake. Hell's bells, it was practically traditional. Up the Mall he went, aiming for the Tube at Charing Cross.

Admiralty Arch loomed. He approached – went through it.

Jesus Christ! What was going on?

There were eighty thousand people in Trafalgar Square – protesting against the United States' military involvement in Vietnam – and **it** was in the air.

Eighty thousand people!

Eighty thousand angry people – with banners and placards – and Vanessa Redgrave – stood between him and his circumcised dick's desire.

Then all of a sudden this mass of humanity moved.

Victor was swept along, in the wrong direction, and the next thing he knew he was taking part in the storming of the American Embassy in Grosvenor Square. Paint and stones were being hurled. Police and protesters were trading punches. There were charging policemen on foot. There were charging policemen on horseback. There were charging protesters, using banners as battering rams. There were cordons. There were skirmishes. There were officers bringing down fleeing protesters with rugby tackles, crashing into the shrubs and daffodils. There was screaming and shouting and fear and fury and pain. There was panic and pandemonium and blood.

The ittishness of his baby daughter's birth was nothing compared to this.

"My God," thought Victor, "this is no dinner party. This is war. This really is **it**!"

Or was it? Compared to the Tet Offensive, this was a dinner

party. In fact, it was practically a quilting bee. Where were the guns? Where were the bodies?

Then it crossed Victor's mind that if the protesters really did succeed in breaking through the cordon of fresh-faced bobbies protecting the embassy steps, and broke into the building, they would find out soon enough where there were guns. And then there would be bodies. In fact, the potential for bodies was stunning.

Hard man Victor was fucked if he was going to get himself shot in some poxy demonstration in Grosvenor Square. He had unfinished business to attend to. There was the future of English literature to consider. He had responsibilities. He had ...... "Oh shit!"

He saw a young protester with a brick, about to bring it down on a policeman's head. The policeman had lost his helmet. He had bright orange hair and a skull that would crack like an egg. Victor grabbed the young protester by the wrist and took the brick away.

"Hey, man," said the protester, "whose fucking side are you on?"

"Are you a cretin – or what?" was Victor's reply.

As he moved swiftly off, as swiftly as the melée would permit, he heard the protester complain: "Hey, did you see that? That pig-fucker stole my brick."

Another policeman spotted Victor holding the brick in his hand, and, assuming that Victor was about to use it, moved in fast, with truncheon raised. Victor dropped the brick, blocked the blow, picked the policeman up and threw him into a bush. All of a sudden, people were cheering and clapping him on the back and trying to shake him by the hand.

Suppressing a momentary Lone-Rangerish swaggering feeling, Victor realised that he had to split – but this was easier said than done.

He plunged into the crowd, got an elbow in his face and his nose began to bleed.

He ducked and bobbed, heaved and weaved, dived and rolled, under one horse, got kicked by another horse in the back of the leg, barely felt it, staggered, tripped, went down, came up again, pushed and barged, jumped over a fence and, finally, broke free.

Then he was up and running, unaware that blood was streaming from his nose, splattering his t-shirt as he ran. Up to Oxford Street. Over Oxford Street. Down St.Christopher's Place. Right onto Wigmore Street.

He came to a halt in Regent Street. He was on fire – hornier than ever.

From the B.B.C. building in Langham Place, an elegant woman emerged. She crossed the street, headed his way, stopped at a dark green Beetle, began to get in.

"Excuse me," said Victor.

"Yes?" Then she noticed the blood. "Are you alright?"

"You're not a hooker by any chance?"

"Get lost, creep," said the woman, climbed into her car, locked the doors, drove off, burning rubber.

His nose stopped bleeding. A taxi passed. He flagged it down. The driver did not know that Victor's t-shirt was meant to be white. He didn't think his passenger was blood-stained. He would not have stopped to pick him up if he had. He thought that Victor's t-shirt was tie-dyed and put him down for a hippy. Had he known, Victor would have been livid.

"Where to, mate?"

"Maida Vale."

"Which end?"

"North."

"I'll go round the park," said the driver.

"Whatever."

Victor sank back into the seat and stared blankly out of the window, as the taxi trundled round Regent's Park, past the zoo, then made a right, and a left, and a right again onto St.John's Wood High Street.

Victor sat up with a start as it dawned on him where he was. He peered out of the window, counting down the shops.

"Hey, wait a minute. Stop!"

"What's up?" asked the driver, stopping.

His father's delicatessen was gone. It was gone. It wasn't there any more. It was gone. A commercial estate agent's sign outside told him that the place had been sold.

"Wait a second," said Victor. "I'll be right back."

He hopped out of the cab, staggered, as an exquisite pain shot up the back of his right leg. He gritted his teeth, went to look in the window, pressed his nose against the glass. It was dark and empty inside.

It was dark and empty inside.

Victor was suddenly overwhelmed by a powerful craving for latkes. In moments of stress a person's stomach goes back to its roots – apart from which, he was starving. Then he caught sight of his t-shirt, reflected in the glass. "Oh my God. Oh dear. Oh shit." He pulled his Levi jacket close about him, took a deep breath, held it, exhaled slowly, turned and made it back to the cab.

"Drive on."

The cab drove on.

Victor did not seem to have a wound. He couldn't find one. Perhaps it was someone else's blood. Yes. That made sense. There'd surely been a lot of it about.

The cab came to a halt at the junction of Carlton Hill and Maida Vale. The intersection of sex and shopping was moments away. But somehow, suddenly, other emotions seemed to be holding sway.

"This alright for you?" asked the cabbie.
"Listen," said Victor, "I've changed my mind."
"Oh yes?"
"Take me to Melrose Avenue."
"Melrose Avenue?"
"Just up from Willesden Green."
"I know it."
"OK?"
"If you can pay, it's OK."
"I can pay."

What with Victor's libido's recession, he had some cash to spare.

So – Maida Vale, which turns into Kilburn High Road, which turns into Shoot-Up Hill, which turns into Cricklewood Broadway – and where Shoot-Up Hill and Cricklewood Broadway meet, left onto Walm Lane. And there was Melrose Avenue: straight ahead.

The taxi stopped outside his parents' house.

Victor paid, clambered out. Pain shot up his leg.

The taxi turned on a sixpence and disappeared.

Victor pushed back the gate, hobbled up the path and rang the bell.

A rabbi came to the door.

"Yes?"

"Oh no," said Victor, feeling himself about to come face to face with **it** in its terminal form. Rabbis do not come to your home, do they, unless someone has died.

"Can I help you?" asked the rabbi, in the kind of gentle careful voice one reserves for dealing with potential lunatics.

"I'm the son," Victor explained.

"You're the son?" the rabbi echoed.

"Yeah," said Victor with a sigh, "I'm Victor."

"Victor?" said the rabbi, wondering how to proceed, convinced by now he had a raving nutter on his hands.

"That's me," said Victor, "the prodigal prodigal" – and made a gesture combined with a shrug which, at least, showed the rabbi that this lunatic was Jewish, which wasn't much consolation.

"How can I help you, Victor?"

"Perhaps you'd like to let me in?"

"You'd like me to let you in? A perfect stranger? At this time of night?"

"I'm Victor, for God's sake. I'm the son. I got married."

"Mazel tov."

Victor just could not bring himself to ask the crucial question: which one of his parents was dead?

"We just had a baby."

"I'm pleased for you, Victor, really, but now, I'm going to bed. Good night."

The rabbi tried to shut the door, but Victor put his foot in it.

"Bed? What bed?"

"Victor, you want I should call the police? Take your foot out of my door."

"Your door?"

"Who else's door should it be?"

"It should be my parents' door. That's whose door it should be."

Around about this point, the penny began to drop.

"Victor Abrahams?"

"That was my name."

"Was?"

"It's a long story."

"You're the Abrahams' son?"

"Who else's son should I be? A person doesn't choose whose son he is. If I had my way, I'd be, I don't know, Emanuel Goldenberg's son. What's going on already?"

"Your father told me he didn't have a son."

"That figures."

The rabbi, then, put two and two together. What had occurred became clear. He put Victor in the picture.

The rabbi, whose synagogue was just up the road in Walm Lane, had bought the house from Victor's father in March. The sale was completed at the end of April, and the Abrahams had gone to live in Tel Aviv in May.

All of a sudden, Victor felt ....strangely bereft. He hung his head and sighed. Then pain shot up his leg again and pitched him forward into the rabbi's arms.

The rabbi propped him against the door.

"You better come in."

"I'm OK. I got kicked by a horse."

"A horse already?"

"Yeah."

"And the blood?"

The rabbi pointed at Victor's t-shirt. His jacket had swung open to reveal his gory front.

"It's not mine."

"Where've you been, Victor? In Grosvenor Square?"

"Yeah."

"Oi veh, Victor, you should be ashamed," said the rabbi. "I saw it on the news."

"Now listen, Rabbi, please, don't start with all that ashamed stuff. I've had a hard day. It's been nice talking to you. I have to go."

Victor regained the perpendicular with an effort.

"Victor," said the rabbi, "I've got your parents' address. It's in my office at the schul. Come by – when you're better. I'll give it to you. Bring the family."

"No, forget it."

"You should at least write."

"Rabbi," said Victor, "I'm sorry I bothered you."

"Do I look bothered? Victor, listen, I'm always here – or there. You hear me, Victor? You understand what I'm saying?"

Victor smiled ruefully, shook his head and winced off into the night.

The rabbi shut his door, went to bed and turned out the light.

Limping along, Victor reflected:

"**It** is all very fine, when it makes your blood sing with excitement. **It** is not so great, when it leaves you feeling like shit."

He considered collapsing right there and then on the pavement – and waiting for the Feds to come along and scoop his body up.

"Mind you, on the other hand, come to think of it," thought Victor, "**It** may sometimes be full of shit, but shit is always full of **it**."

"My God," said Victor to himself, "how multi-layered and deep and ittish is that? Is that a maxim, or what? Le Rochefoucauld, eat your heart out. I must get home at once and write **it** down."

He grimaced. He grinned. A second wind kept him on the move. A third, a fourth, a fifth wind. Adrenalin, from some secret ittish store, propelled him on the long journey home.

13

YOKO OR COCO

John Lennon and Yoko Ono were in the presidential suite of the Hilton Hotel in Amsterdam, conducting a bed-in for peace – and James Earl Ray had counted off his first four days in jail, which left him with only ninety-eight years three hundred and sixty-one more days to go.

In the end, Victor and Suzie chose four names, which they put into a hat.

They had been through Withycombe's Dictionary of English Christian Names from Aaron to Zoe and back again, over and over and over again. They had stuck pins in the phone book, pins in the atlas, pins in the index of the A to Z street guide to London. At one point, Zambia Carnaby Blair was seriously on the cards. They bickered and bantered and bitched and shouted and laughed and the longer it went on, the less likely it seemed that they would ever reach a conclusion. The search for a name had turned into a kind of perpetual parlour game. Meanwhile, the baby grew – and the days flicked by at a speed which would have taken James Earl's breath away.

"It's unfair of you," Mary Poppins complained. "The child should know her own name by now. How can she, if she hasn't got one?"

"She's alright," said Suzie, "she thinks her name is baby."

"Baby's not a name," protested Mary.

In point of fact, the baby had a shrewd suspicion that her name was **It**, which was what Victor called her, when no-one was about.

"I'm sick of this," said Jennifer, one day, "it's boring, irresponsible and immature. I'm surprised at both of you. You're not idiots. The child is going to be one year old in two days time. What are you going to sing? Happy Birthday Dear Baby?"

"I have no problem with that," said Victor.

"What do you want us to do, Mum? We can't agree."

"Each one of you writes down your favourite name on a piece of paper. We'll put them in a hat and draw for it."

"What do you think, Victor?" Suzie asked.

Victor considered the existential implications of this method and finally said: "OK."

Yoko was Victor's first choice.

"Yoko? Don't be silly."

Suzie disapproved of Yoko Ono.

"What's wrong with Yoko?"

Victor, on the other hand, approved of Yoko to such an extent, that when he had read about the bed-in for peace in Amsterdam, he sent her the original manuscript of "What Kept Godot".

"Dear Yoko," read the accompanying note, "you might as well have something decent to read while you're saving the world. Regards to John. Love, Victor B.."

He sent it Special D..

"You can't call anyone Yoko."

"Why not? Yoko's called Yoko."

"Well, precisely. Why would you want to name anyone after her?"

"I think she's terrific. She's ...." Victor paused and pondered, searching for a suitably rosy adjective. He imagined Yoko in bed, in the presidential suite, without John. A certain faraway look came into his eye.

"She's .... really real."

"Oh Victor," laughed Suzie, recognising that certain faraway look, "you can't possibly fancy Yoko Ono?"

"We don't have that kind of relationship at all," said Victor, with a sniff. "And anyway, that's not the point. Yoko's an excellent name."

Coco was Suzie's first choice.

"As in Coco Chanel."

"How can you object to Yoko, if you like Coco? Is that ridiculous, or what?"

"Coco's a brilliant name."

"Yeah," sneered Victor, "if you happen to be a clown."

"Yoko Ono isn't a clown?"

Victor's second choice was Martina, to honour Martin Luther King, shot dead in Memphis, three weeks after the baby was born, by James Earl Ray.

The night that Victor heard the news, he stole from his bed, across the landing, and into the nursery, where his unnamed daughter slept in her cot, the cot from which the Porge had climbed all those years ago. He picked his daughter up. He held her far too tight. He whispered in her ear: "I have a dream. I have a dream." And he burst into tears.

Suzie's second choice was Jane, her paternal grandmother's name, Jane Austen's name, Sweet Jane.

Jennifer went to fetch Felix's ancient Panama hat, hanging still on its hook by the conservatory door.

They found Mary Poppins on her bench in the garden, where she sat, with the baby on her lap, reading "By The Pricking of My Thumbs".

"Oh my God," said Victor, "not Agatha Christie. How can you read that crap?"

"I beg your pardon," said Mary. "Go and wash your mouth out with soapy water."

"Pardon my French," said Victor. "But Agatha Christie. Honestly."

"How many Agatha Christies have you read?" Mary Poppins demanded.

"I haven't read any," said Victor, in a perish-the-thought tone of voice.

"Perhaps you should, then," observed Mary. "Agatha Christie has sold more books to more people in more countries than any other author ever known. She is outsold only by Shakespeare and the Bible. How many books have you sold Victor?"

"Touché," said Suzie.

"Just because something sells doesn't mean it's any good," Victor snapped.

"Can we get on with this?" interrupted Jennifer, holding out the hat. "Now, Mary, Victor and Suzie have agreed each to put their two favourite names for the baby into this hat. You must choose. Pick out two names."

"I see," said Mary, patting the baby, "and what are these names?"

Suzie told her the names were Coco, Yoko, Martina and Jane.

"Is this wise?" Mary Poppins wondered.

"Do you have a better idea?" Jennifer wondered back.

Victor and Suzie put their scrunched-up pieces of paper in the hat.

"Actually," said Victor, "come to think of it, you know, I really think I still like Bridget best of all."

"If you want to swap Yoko for Bridget, Victor, that's fine by me," said Suzie, quick as a flash.

"I'm not taking Yoko out, if you're keeping Coco in."

"Will you two stop squabbling!" Jennifer snapped.

Jennifer handed the hat to Mary Poppins, who perched it on the baby's bum.

Mary reached into the hat, pulled out a scrunched-up piece of paper, unscrunched it, read it, scrunched it up again, popped it into a pocket and said: "Jane."

Suzie smiled. Jane was fine.

Victor glowered.

Mary reached into the hat one more time, pulled out a second scrunched-up piece of paper, unscrunched it, read it, rescrunched it, popped it into her pocket and smiled.

"Well?" said grumpy Victor.

Mary returned the hat to Jennifer, hoisted the baby onto her shoulder, stood up, addressed herself to Victor.

"Your daughter – Jane Martina Blair," said Mary, and handed her over. "Her nappy needs changing."

"Pwaw!" exclaimed Victor, getting a whiff, and whipping his nose away.

"That's my girl," said Suzie.

Victor and Suzie and little Jane, held at arm's length, headed off across the lawn, onto the terrace and into the house.

Jennifer breathed a sigh of relief.

"Well, Mary," she said, "thank goodness for that."

"I think I'll go inside and make a nice cup of tea," said Mary, with a smile.

Jennifer smiled back, watched her go, sat herself down on the bench. The sun was warm and pleasant. A bee buzzed up, descendant perhaps of that very bee which introduced her husband to his maker, landed on her cuff. She held her breath. The bee buzzed off.

The hat was on her lap. In it, the two remaining scrunched-up pieces of paper.

She picked one out of the hat, unscrunched it and read: Martina.

She picked the second one out of the hat, unscrunched that too and read: Jane.

"Well, well, well," said Jennifer Perry, softly to herself. "Good old Mary Poppins."

14

BEANBAGS FROM HELL

On Wednesday, the twelfth of March, 1969, George Harrison was busted, Paul McCartney and Linda Eastman were spliced, and Graham Kirby, the thrusting young director of Kirby's Sporting Goods (Wholesale) took delivery – in canny anticipation of the increased demand about to be engendered by the imminent Open, which would be taking place at Lytham St.Anne's in the second week of July – of two thousand dozen golf balls.

On wooden racks, the balls were stacked, six to a box, (waiting to be whacked), in K.S.G.'s ramshackle warehouse in Wembley.

At five-forty-five, on the thirteenth, the Thursday before baby Jane's first birthday, everyone else having gone home, Graham Kirby entered his warehouse with a woman, who unzipped his fly and pulled out his penis.

At five-fifty-one, he entered the woman, having bent her over a crate of athletic supports, yanked up her mini, pulled aside her knickers and, as was his wont, thrust.

At five-fifty-seven, having achieved their little moment of mutual bliss, they shared a cigarette. She had the final puff, dropped it on the floor, trod on it, and kicked it under the palette which was supporting the weight of the athletic supports. The butt came to rest in a nest of straw and tissue, which had been swept under, when it should have been swept up. The butt continued to smoulder.

At six-oh-three, Kirby and the woman left the building.

At six-seventeen – WHOOSH! – inferno time.

Jock straps, stumps and flannels and hats, dart-boards, tennis rackets, football boots and shorts and shirts, croquet mallets, shuttlecocks, a massive consignment of sporting socks, arrows and pucks and ping-pong bats, riding-crops and judo mats.

The fire, like a lunatic genie unleashed from a long-lost lamp, leaped across the warehouse floor and, with pantophagous glee, licked up the wooden racks, and ignited the golf-balls' cardboard boxes.

Suddenly, twenty-four thousand bright white balls were bouncing in the flames.

You had to be there, fully to appreciate the wonder of this sight. But, of course, had you been there, you'd have fried.

The wooden racks, on which the balls were stacked, supported the warehouse's water tank.

When the racks collapsed into the fire, down came the water tank, with a fearsome ripping and twisting of pipe, which caused a flood, which put out the fire, and which left in its steaming smoking wake a nightmarish woebegone mess.

Kirby dined alone, on Friday night, at Swann's, where George Perry now worked four evening shifts a week.

He drank half a bottle of Muscadet with his egg mayonnaise and prawns – and a bottle of Brouilly with his well-done steak chasseur.

"Tell 'im zere's a five pound souplement for well-done steaks," said Thierry Swann, the restaurant's eponymous chef-patron, with an accent so thick you could butter a baguette with it.

"What, seriously?" wondered George.

"You sink all zat extra gas cost nothing?"

Thierry's wife, Mireille, who ran the front-of-house, with an accent every bit as buttery as her husband's, said:

"Don't you dare zay anysing. Ze customer, 'e is always right."

"Au contraire," said Thierry, "ze customer, 'e is always wrong."

Kirby chewed his gloomy way through half the steak, then

pushed the plate away.

George cleared Kirby's table, took the plates to the kitchen, gave them to Saddam, who washed them up.

George returned to the table.

"Can I get you any pudding?"

"Calvados. Large," said Kirby, knocking back the rest of his Brouilly.

"What does 'e want, ze well-done steak, comme dessert?" Thierry wanted to know.

"Calvados."

"Huh, since 'e is a prick, don't give 'im ze good calva. You give 'im ze cooking calva – but you charge 'im for the good calva."

Kirby put his hand into his jacket pocket and pulled out a golf-ball – charred and cracked and sad – unfit for play.

When George returned to the table, bearing the inferior calvados, Kirby held the golf-ball up and said:

"Look at this piece of worthless fucking shit."

The couple at the table next to Kirby asked for their bill – and left.

Kirby knocked back his calvados in one and demanded another.

"Sure you wouldn't like some coffee?" George suggested, amiably.

"Listen," said Kirby, shaking the golf-ball in George's face, "I've got twenty-three thousand nine hundred and ninety-nine more of these worthless dollops of doot. I don't need coffee – I need calvados."

George brought the drink. Kirby grunted a kind of thanks and stared morosely into his glass. He started into picking at the golf-ball's skin.

The last two tables paid and left.

Thierry and Mireille, and Thierry's commis-chef, Nico, went

home, and Saddam followed on soon after, leaving George alone to see the drunkard out.

Kirby removed the golf-ball's skin and began to unravel its innards onto the table.

Standing behind the tiny bar, polishing glasses, observing this interesting process, George began to wish he had a golf-ball to unravel for himself. It seemed like a kind of therapeutic thing to do.

The very first golf-balls were made of wood, but in the early years of the seventeenth century, they moved onto leather stuffed with boiled feathers.

Then came the Gutta Percha era, in which golf-balls were made of Gutta Percha. Gutta Percha, as everyone knows, is the inspissated juice of various trees found chiefly in the Malayan archipelago.

The beginning of the twentieth century introduced a new ball and a new era. It was the invention of a certain Coburn Haskell, a golfer of Cleveland, and Bertram G.Work of the B.F.Goodrich Company. It had a tension-wound rubber thread, miles of it, wrapped around a solid rubber core. A number of varieties of ball appeared in the Haskell's wake, such as the Kempshall and the Silver King, the Spalding and the Dunlop and the Zodiac.

Kirby's ball was a three-part ball, with an outer Balata cup, with moulded dimples, painted and lacquered, then endless yards of rubber band, wrapped around a rubber centre. The rubber centre, small ball within the ball, was not solid. It was filled with H2O.

Kirby looked up and focussed with some difficulty on George.

"Am I keeping you up?" he asked.

"No," George lied.

"Another calvados. Have one yourself."

George had neither the authority nor the experience to give

the man his bill and chuck him out, so he did as he was told.

"Siddown," said Kirby. "Where's your drink?"

"I don't really drink," apologised George, pulling up a chair.

In his befuddled state, Kirby found this concept hard to grasp. He resumed unravelling.

"This is my life," he slurred. "I'm unravelling my life. I'm unravelling the mystery of life. And what is the fucking mystery of life? Hah!" He tore off the last shred of rubber band and produced a squidgy Malteser-sized rubber ball. "Here it is. The mystery of fucking life. Get me a knife."

"Er ....."

"Come on, son, a knife. I need a knife."

George went to the kitchen and returned with a keen and slender knife.

"Hmmm," purred Kirby, taking the knife, "a person could remove a person's heart with a knife like this."

He tested the well-honed Sabatier blade with his thumb, then addressed it to the inner ball – and sliced it open. Water dribbled out.

"Pathetic," said Kirby, and reached for his drink, but did not relinquish the knife.

"How many did you say you've got?" George enquired.

"Two thousand dozen," Kirby groaned.

"What are you going to do with them?"

"Are you trying to be funny?"

George flinched as Kirby's grip tightened on the knife.

"Not at all, not at all," he stammered. "I was just wondering what you were going to do with them."

"What-the-fuck d'you expect me to do with them? I can think of someone's arse I'd like to shove them up, but that's about all they're good for."

"I'll have them," said George, tentatively.

"You? Whadda you want them for? They're worthless."

"Does it matter?"

"I don't suppose it does."

"Well, can I have them?" – hopefully.

"Listen, son, if you're prepared to pick up twenty-four thousand buggered-up golf-balls, and take the fuckers away, you can have 'em."

"How much?" asked George, nervously.

"I'm not fucking paying you to take them away."

"No, I mean, I thought you'd want me to pay you."

Kirby thought this was very funny and guffawed quite a bit.

"I'll tell you what …….. what's your name?"

"George."

"Tell you what, George, you can get me one last glass of this rot-gut calvados of yours and, shit, you can pay for my fuckin' 'orrible dinner as well. How about that? Deal?"

"Deal," said George.

"When?" asked Kirby.

"Tomorrow? Half past ten?"

"I'll be there."

Kirby gave a homicidal leer, up from under his eyebrows, raised the knife like a dagger, paused, pushed back his chair, stood, swayed, rearranged his grip, spun the knife in the air, deftly caught and threw it, with a vicious flick into the golf-ball's guts.

Thud!

Kirby grinned at the quivering knife, grinned at George, fumbled for his wallet, removed a card, presented it, knocked back the calvados in one, shook George by the hand and, with a cheerful parting shot – "Don't forget to give yourself a tip, sucker!" – he staggered off into the night

George pulled the knife out of the table, out of the table-cloth. He inserted a finger into the hole. Perhaps he could take the table-cloth home and ask Mary Poppins if she'd sew it up.

He scooped up a handful of the golf-balls rubbery remains – squeezed. This was a strangely pleasant thing to do.

Then he tidied up, locked up, crossed the road and went to bed.

The following day, he hired a van – and purchased fifty large black heavy duty plastic sacks.

He drove to Wembley in the van and pulled up in front of the warehouse at ten twenty-five.

"Just five more minutes," said George to himself at a quarter to twelve, and at ten to twelve, and at five to twelve.

Kirby came at noon, in his Jag, seemingly none the worse for wear, except for the fact that he hadn't a clue who George was supposed to be.

"What!" he exclaimed, as George, shoring up his sinking heart, explained.

"I what!"

George repeated himself.

"I didn't!"

"You did," George assured him

The side of the warehouse, beside which this was playing out, had a large door for lorries and a small door for human beings. Kirby produced a bunch of keys, selected one, opened the human beings' door, looked inside.

Talk about an expensive fuck. A desolate sea of soggy ash stretched away into the gloom. Stupid bitch. He could see her shoe distinctly, stepping on the cigarette butt and kicking it under the palette.

Kirby shook his head and sighed. It was worse than he remembered from yesterday morning. Far worse. He turned and scrutinised George.

"Go on then, my son. They're no bloody use to me."

"Can you show me where the lights are?" asked practical George.

"There are no lights. They're fucked."

"Have you got a torch?"

"I wonder, you know, at your gall," said Kirby. "There's one in the Jag, in the boot. Help yourself."

George found the torch. Kirby departed, promising to return at six o'clock. George unloaded his sacks and dumped them by the human beings' door, through which he then stepped, torch in one hand, black plastic sack in the other.

Unspeakable squelch featured under his feet. Rancid cavernous murk lurked over his head. The torch's beam picked out one dimpled sphere, then another, then another. He reached down, wishing he was wearing rubber gloves. What venomous alien life-form pulsated inside these spooky eggs? What heinous harvest was he come to garner? His imagination was beginning seriously to run away with him, when arithmetic took over.

He had, approximately, five and a half hours. That was eleven half hours, which was twenty-two quarter hours, which divided into twenty-four thousand at least a thousand times, which meant that he had to bag more than a thousand balls every fifteen minutes. Working on the assumption that there are sixty seconds in a minute, then: three times sixty is a hundred and eighty, and five times a hundred and eighty is – five noughts are nought, and five eights are forty, and five ones are five, plus four from the forty is .... nine hundred. So a thousand balls every nine hundred seconds. Why, no sweat, that's less than a ball every second. No, hold on, that's wrong. It's more than a ball every second. Superman would be hard-pushed to do the business. Well, you'll just have to do what you can.

As it happened, Kirby did not return till half past eight. He didn't, however, find George hard at work. George had made the fatal mistake of sitting down for a breather. He was fast asleep in the back of the van, surrounded by thirty-nine black plastic sacks, which, stuffed with thousands of buggered-up golf-balls, looked like beanbags from hell.

Kirby locked up his warehouse, considered leaving the lad to his sleep, remembered the torch.

"Hey, wake up."

George ached in every joint, some of which were seizing up. He just about came to, remembered where he was and what was going on.

"Where's my torch?"

"Oh .... actually .... it's in the warehouse."

"Well that's a fat lot of bloody good."

"Sorry."

"What did you leave it in there for?"

"The batteries ran out."

"Oh, great."

"Shall I go and find it?"

"Nah, fuck it."

Filthy and damp, George crawled out of the back of the van, jumped down, staggered.

"Is that the lot?" wondered Kirby.

"Fifteen thousand, four hundred and twenty-seven," said George, and slammed the van doors shut,

"So, what's the plot?"

"Pardon me?"

"What are you planning to do with them?"

"Well," said George, with a yawn, "it all depends on my mother."

Kirby looked at George in disbelief.

Then he said: "Go on. Get out of here. Fuck off."

He'd had enough of this strange young man. George drove home to Ifield Road, parked outside the Laundromat underneath his flat. Over the way, Swann's appeared to be busy.

Up the steps, he lugged the thirty-nine sacks.

They covered his threadbare floor. His room became a macabre store. Inside the black plastic, which picked up spooky accents from the night, the contents seemed to move, shift, breathe – beanbags from hell.

George was unimpressed. For the first time in his life, he did not get undressed and change into his jammies. He fell forward onto the bed – and conked out.

15

THE PARADISE OF FOOLS

Birthdays and the like concentrate the mind on absent friends – especially the eternally absent.

In the darkened dining-room, curtains drawn, waiting for the cake, the conundrum that exercised Jennifer Perry's mind was that Felix, had he lived, would have rejoiced in his grandchild – but, had Felix lived, her affair with Hugo might have, would probably have, continued. And where would that have ended up? In the divorce courts? With all the pain and shame which that entailed? No, not divorce. Divorce would not have been an option. Their religion expressly forbad it, and Felix was a stickler for the rules. But separation – separation would have occurred. And then where would she have been? Supposing ...... supposing what? She scrunched this idle speculation up and threw it on the fire.

Never mind what might have been. Here she was. And here came Mary Poppins with the cake.

Baby Jane's face beamed in the lone candle's light. A little hand reached for the flame. Suzie blew the candle out. They all sang: "Happy Birthday" – Suzie, Victor, Jennifer, Tom, George and Mary Poppins.

At which the baby's beaming face faltered, clouded. The corners of her mouth turned down. Her bottom lip extended, quivered. Lachrymal ducts went into production. Jane began to wail.

Victor hoisted her out of her high-chair, gave her a hug.

"Open the curtains. George, there's a good boy," said Jennifer.

Stiff and aching, George arose with a wince, crossed to the curtains and pulled them. Light came in. The baby howled.

"Give her to me," said George, to everyone's surprise.

"OK," said Victor, and handed her over.

George took the baby and rocked her in his arms with exaggerated care.

"Don't worry, Porge," said Suzie, "she isn't going to break."

"I'd just like to make one thing absolutely clear:" said George, as the crying began to die down, "my name is George. I am not a Porge. I am a person."

The crying stopped. Jane looked up at George, focussed through her lingering tears, smiled.

"Well done, George," said Jennifer.

George looked down at Jane. He smiled. He laughed: "She looks just like Edward G. Robinson."

"She does not!" protested Victor. Edward G. Robinson indeed. Emanuella Goldenberg! He looked at his daughter afresh.

"Oh my God," he said, with some alarm, "she does look like Edward G. Robinson!"

"All children look like Edward G. Robinson," said Mary Poppins, looking up from cutting the cake. "It's perfectly normal."

"I didn't," said Suzie.

"No, that's right, you didn't," Jennifer agreed. "When you were a baby you looked like Winston Churchill."

"Thanks, ma."

"So," said Tom, through a mouthful of crumpet, his fourth, "when's the, you know, christening?"

"What christening?" said Victor. "There's not going to be any christening."

"Victor," said Jennifer, "the child will have to be baptised."

"Why?"

"To take away her original sin."

"What original sin?"

"The original sin with which we all are born, Victor. The original sin which prevents us from achieving our true destiny, until such time as we are baptised and introduced to Grace." The ghost of a wicked smile appeared on Jennifer's finely chiselled face. "You could be baptised too – at the same time. I'm sure you'll agree that it's about time you started achieving your true destiny."

This gave Victor pause for thought, but not for the reason Jennifer supposed. The scenario, which instantly revealed itself to Victor's mind's eye, involved him and his daughter being baptised in some nebulous church, with a photographer standing by taking photographs.

CUT TO: The Walm Lane Synagogue and Victor asking the Rabbi for his parents' address in Tel Aviv.

CUT TO: Victor inserting the photographs, eight-by-ten colour glossies, into an envelope – and posting them off.

CUT TO: The Abrahams at home in Tel Aviv – opening the envelope and – "Oi gevalt! What's this!!" – His parents drop down dead. Matricide and patricide in one fell swoop.

"I don't believe in original sin," said Victor. "I think it's an obnoxious doctrine. Look at her, for God's sake!"

All eyes turned to the gurgling Jane, who was as happy as Larry, now, in George's arms.

"Are you honestly trying to tell me," Victor went on, "that my daughter, my beautiful daughter, your beautiful granddaughter, was born with original sin? I simply don't buy into that at all. It's codswallop. The whole point of children is that they don't have sin. They're pure. They're without blot."

"Does anyone want that last crumpet?" wondered Tom.

"Help yourself," said George.

Last crumpet rhymed in Jennifer's mind with Last Trumpet.

"And what about your daughter's immortal soul?" she said.

"What about it?" Victor replied.

"Do you want her to go to limbo when she dies?"

"Mum!" protested Suzie. "This is her first birthday. What are you talking about? She's not going to die."

"We all die sometime, Susan, and if we are not baptised, we go to limbo."

"Limbo," scoffed Victor. "Do me a favour."

"Aaah," said Tom, "the Paradise of Fools."

"What's that?" said Victor, suspiciously. It sounded like a title he should have thought of himself.

"Er," said Tom, peering myopically into his memory bank, "something, something the sport of winds ...... fly o'er the backside of the world ......"

"Backside of the world?" Suzie laughed.

"...... fly o'er the backside of the world into a Limbo large and broad, since called .... The Paradise of Fools."

"Shakespeare?" wondered Mary Poppins.

"John Milton. My man!" said Tom, who, when all was said and done, was the only person in the room with a degree, and a quite respectable one at that.

"Milton Schmilton," Victor muttered, "give us some of that cake."

"How do you remember that stuff?" asked Suzie.

"I don't know," said Tom. "It amazes me."

"Excuse me," said Jennifer, frostily. She pushed back her chair, stood up and left the room.

They all looked after her.

Victor said: "Is she serious, or what?"

Suzie said: "Well of course she is."

George said: "I think this baby's wet."

"Give her to me," said Mary Poppins.

George gave Jane to Mary, and Mary took her away.

"Is it alright to smoke a joint?" asked Tom.

"No, it's not," said Suzie.

"Suze?" Victor wondered.

"What?"

"You don't buy into all this original sin baloney, do you?"

"Who? Me?"

"Yes. You."

"No. No, I don't. I mean, it doesn't make sense ...... does it?"

"How about limbo?"

Suzie frowned. The thought of limbo, clearly, caused her some concern.

"Who knows?" she said – and shrugged.

George pushed back his chair, stood up and left the room.

"I think I'll just take a stroll round the garden," said Tom, with a wink, and followed him out.

Jennifer sat at the kitchen table, straight-backed, absently wringing her hands in her lap, staring, thinking, gnawing at this particular bone, which most of the time remained buried:

"If Felix was alive ...... if Felix was alive, he'd know how to deal with Victor. He'd have known how to negotiate. If Felix was alive, who knows, Suzie might never have married a penniless Godless Jewish writer, however strangely charming he might be. If Felix was alive, he'd have certainly received his knighthood by now, and I'd have been Lady Perry. But that's nothing, no, and, well, and here we go again, if Felix was alive, we'd have been separated, and I wouldn't be here and .... And then, if Felix was alive today, he'd be, my goodness, almost seventy years old. Oh Lord, he might even be dead. Oh dear, this is nonsense. And how could he have coped with it all, his children, his glorious children – a shop-girl and a waiter? He wouldn't have liked it. He wouldn't have liked it at all."

Suzie was working at the Apple boutique, a commercially suspect, but otherwise delightful psychedelic store on Baker Street. It was great fun, and handy, because it meant that she and Victor could travel into work together on the tube. They would kiss goodbye at Baker Street station. Then he would head off to Primrose Hill on foot, and she would float down the road.

George, in fact, had two jobs. He worked four nights a week at Swann's. And, by day, he was now a trainee estate agent and worked for North and Hillard. But it was the being-a-waiter in any shape or form that caused his mother distress.

Jennifer took a deep breath, put her elbows on the table, her head in her hands, and sighed.

"Mum?"

She looked up.

"Oh, hello George."

"Can I have a word?"

"What's on your mind?"

He crossed the red and black checkerboard lino floor and sat himself down at the kitchen table opposite his mother. Behind her, through the kitchen window, he could see Tom, in the garden, puffing away at a furtive spliff.

"Mum," said George, narrowing his eyes to concentrate, "how much did it cost to send Suzie to Sussex?"

"Good Lord," said Jennifer, with a small laugh. Talk about a bolt from the blue. "Why do you ask?"

"How much? Three – four – five thousand pounds? More?"

"What does it matter?"

"If I had been clever, and I'd got into university, would you have paid for me to go as well?"

"Of course."

"And you'd have been able to afford it?"

"We'd have managed."

"And would you still be able to manage it now?"

"Why George, you dark horse," said Jennifer, surprise and delight illuminating her patrician features, "don't tell me you've gone and got yourself into a university."

"Would you be able to afford it?"
"I could afford it. Oh, darling, I'm so pleased. Where did you get in?"
"I didn't get in anywhere."
"But I thought you said ……"
"Mum, I've got one A-level. Just."
"Then what was all that about?"
"I just wanted to establish that you can afford it."
"Why?"
"Because I want my money."
"What money?"
"The money you would have spent on me, if I had got in."
"But you didn't."
"Look, Mum, I need two thousand pounds."
"George?"
"What?"
"Are you in trouble?"
"How would I be in trouble?"
"I've no idea. Are you?"
"No, I'm not. I just need two thousand pounds."
"What for?"
"Business."
"Business? You don't know anything about business."
"Mum, I need two thousand pounds – and I'll pay you back in six months, with ten per cent interest."
"Are you sure you're not in trouble?"
"Would you like me to swear on the Bible?"
"That won't be necessary."
"It's really a much better deal than if I had got into some university. It's less of a capital outlay, overall. And you get paid back – and you make a profit. Ten per cent."
"Well, well, well. Perhaps you do know something about business after all."

"I've been paying my rent and all my own bills for a year and a half, which is more than can be said for certain other people I could mention."

"Point taken," said Jennifer. She sat back in her chair and considered her son anew.

George met her eyes for a moment, then looked away over her shoulder, through the kitchen window, just in time to catch sight of Tom, as, whoops, he tripped on the garden hose, which snaked across the lawn, and disappeared with suddenness from view.

"Assuming for the moment that I could advance you this enormous sum, what happens if you don't pay me back?"

"I will pay you back."

"Yes, but just suppose that for some reason you can't. What can you offer me by way of collateral?"

"Well, said George, "you can take it out of my inheritance."

Jennifer smiled: "I see you've thought this out."

"I have."

"I'll give you one thousand pounds."

"I need two."

"Fifteen hundred. And that's my final offer. Deal?"

George bit his bottom lip, frowned, made calculations in his head, grinned.

"Deal," said George.

He stood up and, with a certain pleasurable formality, shook his mother's hand.

"You won't regret this, Mum."

"I trust not."

Tom rolled onto his back and stared up at the sky. Gravity pinned him down.

High overhead, heading for the reservoir, a squadron of Canada geese flew between him and the sun and honked in gravity's face.

16

COSMIC BALLS

"Houston. Tranquillity Base. The Eagle has landed," said Neil Armstrong.

The early hours of Monday morning, July 21, 1969 – were you up and glued to your set? George wasn't. George was fast asleep in Ifield Road.

Victor and Suzie and baby Jane were up and watching at Number Nine – while Mary and Jennifer slept.

In Thurloe Square, on LSD, Tom was having trouble with his telly, which seemed to be melting.

At 3.56 am, British Summer Time, Neil Armstrong stepped off the ladder of the lunar module, Eagle, onto the moon.

The moon!

Now there's a cosmic golf-ball, if ever there was – sliced out of sight in the course of some divine competition, lost in the intergalactic rough.

The Gods play golf. Of course they do. They love to whack a planet. Wouldn't you? Nothing at all can beat the thrill of getting a black-hole-in-one. Well, what else did you think black holes were for?

On the twenty-fourth, the astronauts returned to earth – as did Tom.

"This is the greatest week in the history of the world since the Creation," said the President of the United States of America, a man called Richard Milhous Nixon.

"Oh yes?" said a tight-lipped Mary Poppins. "Tell that to the children who are starving to death in Biafra."

As far as George was concerned, the greatest week in the history of the world since the Creation was the week he paid his mother back, with interest, and earned about a million Brownie points into the bargain.

George was selling his balls at ten shillings a throw.

They were painted black, by Saddam and Saddam's friend, Hussein. He paid them a penny a ball.

Each ball was placed in a very smart, silver cardboard, sugared-almond box. The boxes, an over-geared Northern confectioner's bankrupt stock, were purchased by George from the Receiver for a song. They worked out at just under thruppence a piece.

The labels were printed in Clerkenwell. They were sticky labels. George stuck them on himself. That is to say, he, himself, stuck them on the boxes.

"Cosmic Ball," said the labels. "Unravel the Mystery of Life."

"Far out," said Tom. "How much?"

"Ten bob."

Tom coughed up and became the first human being on the planet to purchase a Cosmic Ball.

"This is great," he said, unravelling away. "I could sell hundreds of these."

George offered him ten per cent commission.

Tom persuaded George to place the following advertisement in OZ, I.T., Private Eye, Time Out, the NME and Penthouse Magazine:

"Question: What has Howard Hughes been doing all these years?

"Answer: Unravelling Cosmic Balls.

"You too can unravel the Mystery of Life for only ten shillings. Send your cheque or postal order to Cosmic Balls, c/o the C.I.A., P.O.Box No.666, London SW10."

"Don't you think he might object?"

"Who?"

"Howard Hughes."

"It would be great publicity if he does."

"I don't like it," said George, worrying. "At least let's drop the C.I.A. – that's just asking for trouble."

"Church of the Infant Adam."

"What?"

"Trust me," said Tom, "I'm in advertising."

This was somewhat stretching the point. Tom was working, in Soho's periproctal parts, as a messenger for V.P.L., the commercials production company: "Eleven pounds a week and you have to provide your own car."

But, credit where credit is due, the advertisement worked. Cheques and postal orders began to appear on the mat.

At the end of August, Tom persuaded George to disguise himself as a hippy and accompany him to the Isle of Wight, where, among others, Bob Dylan would be playing his first concert in three years, after his near fatal motorcycle crash.

They took four hundred Cosmic Balls between them.

Cannabis clouds wafted over makeshift tents and naked painted bodies. Rock and Roll. Tom was in his element, grinning from ear to ear and peddling Cosmic Balls, with a wink, at double the recommended retail price.

George, looking like an undercover cop, summoned all his courage up, targeted a likely-looking hippy, who was in fact an undercover cop, and attempted to sell him his wares.

The next few minutes were something of a blur.

Policemen popped up from nowhere and carried him off.

The constabulary were convinced that George's Cosmic Balls contained some kind of illegal drug.

Down at the hoosegow in Newport, Detective Inspector Littleboy refused to believe that Cosmic Balls were nothing more than buggered-up golf-balls, painted black. And having made Constable Beckett unravel half a dozen, he further refused to believe that the liquid in the ball within the ball was nothing but water – and sent them off to the lab to be analysed.

Back at Number Nine, Victor and Suzie had the house to themselves. Mary Poppins had taken the baby off for the afternoon. Jennifer was playing bridge in Chiswick.

"What now?" said Victor.

"Let's fuck," said Suzie.

"Oh, if you insist."

"I do. I do."

So, there they were, fucking away, and it was all extremely pleasant, when Suzie said: "I haven't taken my pill."

"Pardon?"

"You heard. Oh, please don't stop."

"You could get pregnant."

"I know. Wouldn't that be nice?" purred Suzie, locking her long legs behind his back and holding him in.

"Are you crazy? You just had a baby."

"I want another one," she said and, reaching underneath, squeezed his (cosmic) balls.

Down below, the phone began to ring.

"Saved by the bell," said Victor.

"Ignore it," said Suzie, squeezing.

Victor withdrew from his wife with a struggle, grabbed a gown, ran downstairs and answered the phone.

"Victor, it's me, George."

"Hello, George, what can I do for you?"

"I've been arrested."

"No!"

"Honestly. I have. They think I injected my balls with LSD."

At this, Victor hooted into the phone.

"Hey, what's so funny? Victor, pay attention. I'm in jail."

"Where are you?"

"The Isle of Wight."
"Are you innocent?"
"Well of course I'm innocent. Now, listen, Victor, I haven't got much time. You have to get some press down here before they let me go."
"How do you suggest I do that?"
"Phone them up."
"Phone who up?"
"The press, Victor. The newspapers. Listen, I'll make it worth your while. Phone the NME. Tell them I'm an advertiser. Phone the ……."
The phone went dead.
"George? George?"
Victor hung up.
Enter Suzie, with nothing on.
"Come back to bed, Victor. Right this minute."
"That was George. He's been busted. He's inside."
"The Porge? In prison? I don't believe it."
George's brain seemed to be working well under pressure. Of course, he knew he wasn't guilty, which helped. And it never even occurred to him that he might be framed. It was a simple misunderstanding. George approved of the police. He had been brought up to believe that policemen were his friends. He was on their side. They were on his side.
He sat in his cell, imagining headlines and the subsequent dramatic upturn in Cosmic Ball sales, waiting for the laboratory results, hoping that Victor would have some success and that the press would arrive before he was released.
Tom was supposed to rendez-vous with George at half past five at Harvey's Hot Dog Stand. He had sold all his balls, bought some dope, and ambled up to the stand at half past six, well pleased with himself, his tassled buck-skin shoulder-bag bulging with cash. He hung about for half an hour, then

ambled off again into the heaving throng, which was a hundred and fifty thousand strong.

"Oh well," thought Tom, "I'll catch up with him later."

George fell asleep in his cell. He had a nightmare. He dreamed he was asleep in his cell and he peed in his pants in his sleep. Then he woke up, in his dream, and the cell was full of reporters and photographers, all pointing at his pee-soaked pants, taking photographs and laughing.

He woke up in real life. The cell was empty. He was dry. Thank God! Oh, thank you, God. He peed in the pot provided for this purpose – went back to sleep.

Constable Beckett came at half-past seven and gave him a cup of tea and bacon sandwich.

"Are there a lot of people waiting to see me?"

"What kind of people?"

"Photographers? Reporters? You know – the Press."

"Who do you think you are?" said Constable Beckett – and left.

Littleboy turned up at half past ten.

"Alright, Perry, hop it."

"Do you mean that I am free to go?"

"Don't get clever with me, son. Piss off."

"What about my balls?"

"Don't tempt me, Perry."

Littleboy looked down at his heavily toe-capped shoe. George followed his train of thought. A toe-cap like that could inflict serious testicular damage.

"But ...."

"Your balls, Perry, have been confiscated. They are offensive weapons."

"No they're not."

"Oh yes they are. They are offensive weapons. They are just the kind of thing that hippies throw at policemen. They are offensive."

"But they're my property. You can't do that."

Littleboy gave George a ghastly mirthless smile and hissed: "Oh yes I can."

All of a sudden, it dawned on George that he had strayed into a realm, where the rules as he had been taught them somehow did not apply.

He got out of there as fast as he could, only to be greeted by nobody at all. On the mobilising-the-press front, Victor had scored a big fat zero. Of Tom and the Moke, there was no sign.

Sometimes, when he was younger, in the summer, George would do a thing which he called "shrinking the world". He would lie on his back on the grass and shut his eyes. Then he would imagine that he was not simply lying on the grass, but that he was lying on the planet – which of course he was. He would imagine the whole vast planet underneath his back. Then he would shrink it, slowly, till he felt the curve of it under his spine, till it was smaller than him, and smaller – to the size of an orange, to the size of a pea, to the size of a peppercorn. And there he would be, supported in space by this peppercorn planet. Then he would make the planet altogether disappear. And there he would then be, vastness now personified, a planet in his own right, with his own moon, majestic and serene, floating in space.

Homeward bound, in the train, in his hippy gear, George underwent the very opposite effect. He experienced maximum smallness. He dwindled away inside. He was smaller than an orange. A pea was larger and more effective than him. And he was shrinking. A peppercorn? He was a crumb. If the train had not pulled into the station when it did, he might well have altogether disappeared.

It was a sad and bedraggled George who trudged his weary way from Earl's Court Tube to Ifield Road, climbed the steps and fumbled for his keys.

"George Perry?"

The voice was American. George turned to see an amiable, fit and clean-cut crew-cut man, carrying a Samsonite attaché case and wearing a dark blue suit, with a white button-down shirt and a black knitted tie, smiling up at him.

"Yes," George admitted, long-sufferingly.

"Cosmic Balls?"

"What about them?"

"I have a business proposition I'd like to put to you, if I might come inside."

Looking over his interlocutor's shoulder, George noticed another crew-cut in a blue suit with a white button-down shirt and a black knitted tie. This one was twice as big as the first one, wearing dark glasses and leaning back against an unmarked van.

"Er ....," said George, suddenly terribly aware of his exceedingly un-businesslike apparel.

"I can assure you, Mr Perry, that it would be to your advantage if you would be so kind as to spare me a moment or two of your most valuable time."

"OK," said George, "come in. You'll have to excuse my ridiculous get-up. I've been at a, er, fancy dress party."

George opened the door and led the way upstairs. Reaching the top of the stairs, it occurred to him to wonder how on earth this man had found his name and address. Neither featured in any of the advertisements. There was a Post Office Box Number (666), which was supposed to protect him.

"How did you find me?"

"Ways and means, George. Ways and means."

George inserted his key in the door of his room.

The stacks and stacks and stacks of tiny silver boxes gave the room a rather festive air, more like Santa's grotto than some discotheque in hell.

"Tea?" asked George, picking up a bottle of milk and giving it a cautious sniff.

"No, thank you. May I sit down?"

"Oh, sorry, yes, help yourself."

The man gestured to George that he should also be seated.

George sat. The man sat.

"What's your name?" asked George, as though he had already been told it and somehow it had just slipped his mind.

"You can call me Hank."

"Oh, Hank. Well, Hank, what's all this about?"

"I represent certain interests, George, who would like to .... buy your balls."

"Oh really? How many were you after?"

"All of them, George. All of them."

"I see, well, that's fantastic. I mean, I could probably do you quite a good discount."

"No, no, George, this is not a negotiation. This is a one-way deal."

Hank reached his hand inside his jacket, in the manner of a man who is about to produce a gun and shoot you straight between the eyes.

Mercifully, this did not occur. Rather, the man, Hank, produced a key, lifted the Samsonite case onto the table, unlocked and opened it.

George boggled. The case was full of money.

"I have been authorised," said Hank, "to offer you ten thousand English pounds for your entire stock of Cosmic Balls."

There were twenty packets of ten pound notes inside the case. Hank removed them, one by one, and placed them on the table as he spoke.

"There are, however, certain conditions."

"Oh yes?" said George, swallowing hard.

"You relinquish all rights to and in Cosmic Balls, effective as of now? Understand?"

"Yes. Absolutely."

"You cease to use the letters C.I.A. in any business venture whatsoever, ever."

"It was a joke."

"Not funny, George."

"Church of the Infant Adam."

"Blasphemous too, George. That's bad."

"Sorry."

"And you never use the name of Howard Hughes in any kind of promotional or advertising material. Is that clear?"

"Crystal."

"I don't have to repeat any of that?"

"No more Cosmic Balls. No more C.I.A. No more Howard Hughes."

"Finally, George, this transaction and the conditions of this transaction are not for public consumption. You will not breathe a word of this to any living soul. Agreed?"

"Agreed."

"Very good. We have a deal then?"

"Where do I sign?"

"You don't. This, George, is a gentleman's agreement. It is not anticipated you will break it."

"Don't you want a receipt?"

"That won't be necessary."

Hank then summoned his side-kick and together they removed the remaining thirteen thousand, four hundred and sixty-three Cosmic Balls and stowed them in the unmarked van, while George, his head in a spin, peppered them with questions, as up and down the stairs they came and went.

Were they Mormons? Did they work for Howard Hughes? Had they met Howard Hughes? What was he like? Or did they work for the C.I.A, and had Howard Hughes asked the C.I.A. to make the approach? And where were the Cosmic Balls going? What were they going to do with them? Were they going to destroy them, or what? Were they actually going to be taken to Howard Hughes, stashed aboard some military plane and rushed to wherever he was? Is that what this was all about? Did Howard Hughes, in fact, really want to unravel the Mystery of Life?

To these and other questions, Hank did not respond.

17

THE GREATEST STORY EVER TOLD

On a fresh sheet of paper, Victor wrote the following words:

"The Greatest Story Ever Told"
by
Victor Blair

So there it was, the title page.
Now all he had to do was ....

18

VOODOO & VACANT POSSESSION

George put in an offer on a flat-fronted, tall and narrow, terraced house in Hollywood Road.

Craven, his boss at the North and Hillard office where he worked, told him that the offer was absurd. It may have been absurd, but the offer was accepted.

Yes! It was accepted.

Acceptance, exchange, completion – and the place was his. Hooray! Well, not quite hooray. He did not have vacant possession.

The house had four floors and was divided up into four small flats – basement, ground, first and top. The ground and top floors were empty.

In the basement, there lived an aspiring musician, one Quentin "Call-me-Q." von Muesel

In the light of his encounter with Hank, George had expanded his wardrobe, and when he knocked on the basement door, he was wearing a dark blue suit and a white button-down shirt with a black knitted tie.

Quentin von Muesel was extremely tall and extremely thin and had an extremely deep voice.

"Yeah?" he said, suspiciously, opening the door no more than a crack.

"Mr von Muesli?" George inquired.

"Muesel. Von Muesel."

"Mr von Muesel, my name is George Perry. I've just bought

this building and I have a proposition I would like to put to you. May I come in?"

"What kind of a proposition?"

"One that would be to your advantage. May I come in?"

Von Muesel retreated into the basement, and George followed him in, wrinkling his fastidious nose.

The lanky musician crossed to a mattress in the middle of the floor, at either end of which towered two monolithic speakers. He subsided onto the mattress, pulled his guitar onto his lap, and started to strum. His extremely long hair fell forward and his face became invisible.

"Mr von Muesel ......"

"Call me Q. – everyone does."

George reached inside his jacket and pulled out a packet of fifty one-pound notes.

There was a table and a chair in the room. George pulled out his handkerchief, (he always carried a hanky) dusted down the seat of the chair, sat and pulled himself up to the table.

There was a hookah on the table and a chillum and a bong. George was not so innocent these days that he did not recognise drug paraphernalia when it stared him in the face. For a brief moment, George considered simply calling the police and having the man arrested. But no, he proceeded with Plan A, pushed aside a pile of Furry Freak Brothers comics and started to count out the money, note by note, onto the table, as he spoke:

"Well, Q., how would you like to earn fifty pounds?"

"How?"

"By leaving."

"You want me out?"

"Yes."

"You're going to give me fifty quid to go?"

"That's right."

Q. looked up from his guitar and pondered for a beat or two

the Jimi Hendrix poster, which was blue-tacked to the wall behind George's head.

"Fifty quid?"

"That's what I said."

"OK."

This somewhat took the wind out of George's sails. He had been expecting a battle. The man's passivity perplexed him.

"Will you be alright?" he asked, a victim of lingering scruples.

"Do you care?"

George did not reply, because, when he came to think of it, he didn't.

Two days later, Q. was packed up and gone, heading for some distant rock and roll Valhalla.

In the first floor flat, Mrs Brenda Russell was an altogether different proposition. A widow, spruce and seventy years old, she was utterly indifferent to George's Hankish modus operandi.

"You can keep your money. I don't want it."

"I'll find you another flat," suggested George, thinking he could ship the biddy out and install her in his room in Ifield Road.

"I don't want another flat. This is my home."

And indeed it was. It was neat and tidy. There were antimacassars and Toby jugs and Busy Lizzies and photographs in frames of her and her late husband, Harold, at different happy stages of their life.

"I'll pay my rent, as I've always done. Now go away," said doughty Mrs Russell.

He went away and wandered off and wondered what to do. Couldn't he, by rights, just throw the baggage out? But even if he could, he couldn't, if you see what I mean – could he? I mean, George was not a gangster. He was a nice English middle-class boy – wasn't he? And he wouldn't throw an old lady out onto the street – would he?

He went to see his sister, who in the wake of the Apple Shop's demise was now working at Biba in High Street Ken.

"Hi there, Porge, how's it hanging?"

"I've just bought a house."

"Oh," said Suzie, taken aback, "what kind of a house?"

"A very nice house, in Hollywood Road."

Suzie would have loved to buy a house. However, in Victor's book (not the one he was failing to write) Number Nine was fine. It suited him down to the ground – and hadn't it been suiting her down to the ground as well? Well, yes, it had. But somehow or other, she had of late, though wherefore she knew not, lost all her mirth. And somehow or other, things just did not seem to be going according to plan, although, in point of fact, there was no plan, as such, but, even so ....

"I need someone to help me do it up," said George.

"Oh yes?" said Suzie, failing to keep an edge of bitterness out of her voice. "David Hicks?"

"How about Susan Perry .... sorry .... Susan Blair?"

"Me?"

"Why not? I'll pay you forty pounds a week."

When she came to think about it, leaving aside the strangeness of working for one's strait-laced younger brother, it really was a more than somewhat tempting proposition. Suzie jumped at the idea and handed in her notice.

"See, what I want," said George, as he showed his sister round the house, "is to turn the basement and the ground floor into one flat, and the first floor and the top floor into another flat. We'll have to do the bottom flat first, while I work out what to do with Mrs Russell."

He moved out of Ifield Road and into the top flat, from which he removed the carpets. Then he bought a pair of tap dancing shoes from Anello and Davide and took to pacing up and down late at night, rap-a-tap-a-tap-a-tap, in principle on top of Mrs Russel's skull. But all that Mrs Russell had to do was remove her hearing-aid, and the tarantellas on her ceiling disappeared. So, that was a waste of time.

He upped the ante to one thousand pounds, but Mrs Russell wasn't having any of it.

He bought a ticket for a cruise to Dubrovnik. He typed up a note, which read: "Congratulations, Mrs Russell, you have won a free cruise in the National Sweepstake Travel Lottery. Enjoy your trip." When she went on the trip, he would have all her stuff removed, and change the locks. He put the ticket and the letter in an envelope. "See Dubrovnik and die," he muttered, and slipped it under her door. But Mrs Russell did not hold with "abroad" and bunged the letter and the ticket in the bin.

He lied. He said he needed the flat for his mother, an invalid, who only had a very short time to live.

"Then she shouldn't be up here on the first floor, should she, Mr Perry?"

"No, you don't understand, my mother's going to be downstairs, but we need this flat desperately for her team of round the clock nurses."

"It sounds to me as though your poor unfortunate mother ought to be in a home – far more comfortable."

"Well, surely, it would be far more comfortable for you to be in a home, Mrs Russell. It can't be much fun for you, trudging up and down these stairs all day long."

"The stairs keep me healthy, Mr Perry. Fit as a fiddle I am, thanks to those stairs. And when I get my telegram from the Queen, it'll be those stairs I have to thank for it. And I'll thank you to leave me alone. Good day." And she slammed the door in his face.

Jesus wept, surely not. The old bat could not possibly be planning to live to a hundred!

Voodoo was Victor's idea.

It was Christmas at Number Nine, and George bought Jane some plasticine as a present.

After the turkey and stuffing and Brussel sprouts and Christmas pudding and brandy butter and mince pies, George found Victor in the conservatory, fashioning tiny figures out of the plasticine.

"What are you doing?" asked George.

"I'm attempting to eliminate some of the competition," Victor explained, reaching for a knitting needle, left behind by Mary Poppins on one of the Lloyd Loom chairs.

He aimed the knitting needle at the three pathetically childish plasticine people laid out on the tessellated conservatory floor.

"Say goodbye," said Victor, with three vicious stabs, "to Joseph Heller, Gore Vidal and Norman fucking Mailer."

Stab! – stab!! – stab!!!

It was one thing, **deciding** to write "The Greatest Story Ever Told" – but actually writing it, that was another thing altogether.

"I see," said George, "if you can't join 'em, kill 'em."

"I don't know," said Victor with a sigh, and shook his handsome head. "I really don't know."

And he really didn't.

George bided his time. There was still a chance that the Asian flu might do for Mrs Russell.

Influenza due to the Hong Kong A2 virus killed 2,850 people in Britain in the week ending January 9, the highest weekly figure since 1933. In the week ending December 26, there were 1,421 deaths, with 731 on Christmas and Boxing Day, and 2,400 in the following week. Nearly seven thousand people, many of them old, met their Maker over the festive season.

But Mrs Russell, dammit, seemed to be immune.

Come the end of January, George gave up hope and bought himself a couple of plain white candles and some pins.

Up on the top floor of Hollywood Road, he lit the candles, melted down the wax, and with the melted wax effected an effigy of poor old Mrs Russell.

He waited for midnight, and with its chiming, plunged twelve pins into the effigy's heart.

"Die – Brenda – Russell – die – die – die. Die – Brenda – Russell – die – die – die."

As George intoned these horrifying words, he was almost horrified to find himself not horrified, but thrilled, to think that down below, beneath his feet, a woman was being killed.

It is only minutely to George Perry's credit, that he breathed a sigh of relief, when, on the stairs the following morning, he met Mrs Russell – alive and kicking and chipper as ever.

Imagine, though, George's consternation, later that morning, when he read on the front page of his Daily Telegraph that, during the night, the great philosopher, Bertrand Russell, had died.

Chinese voodoo whispers. Spooky Satanic crossed lines. The confusion of Brenda with Bertrand was easily done. Never mind that the author of "History of Western Philosophy", the passionate searcher for truth and justice and love, was ninety-seven years old – George just could not help but think that he had killed the old bugger. It was a heavy burden to bear, being the man who murdered Bertrand Russell.

Still, things in the end turned out rather well, because on the day before Jane's second birthday, Mrs Russell tripped on a kerbstone at the junction of Fulham Road and Cavaye Place – and broke her hip. And, this being the case, she decided to leave Hollywood Road and go to live with her sister in her sister's bungalow in deepest Cheam.

For Victor, though, things were getting worse. Never mind

the Virgin Birth, never mind the star in the East or the West or the North or wherever it was, dear old Victor was still bogged down in the dawn of fucking creation, attempting to put down on paper that which no-one had ever succeeded in putting down on paper before – **it**.

"I mean," he said, "I know writing's supposed to be difficult. But does it have to be this difficult?"

Then, on the actual day of Jane's second birthday, the sixteenth of March, 1970, the Oxford and Cambridge University Presses published the New English Bible and sold one million copies. The bastards! They sold one million copies on that very first day – then started reprinting at the rate of twenty thousand a week!

"I mean," thought Victor, "what is the point?"

19

MORE SEX & SHOPPING

Round and round the Rings of Satan go.

Ohio. Kent State University. National Guard open fire. Four human beings dead.

Israel. Lebanese border. Rocket attack on school bus. Twelve human beings dead.

Spain. British Comet crashes. One hundred and twelve human beings dead.

Peru. Plane crash. Ninety-nine human beings dead.

Cairo. Nasser's funeral. Mob stampede. Forty-six human beings dead.

Australia. Melbourne. West Gate Bridge collapses. Thirty-three human beings dead.

Philippines. Typhoon. Eight hundred human beings dead.

France. St.Laurent-du-Pont. Dance hall fire. One hundred and forty-six human beings dead.

East Pakistan. Typhoon and tidal wave. More than one hundred and fifty thousand human beings dead.

Poland. Gdansk. Two days of rioting. Six human beings dead.

Scotland. Glasgow. Ibrox Park football barriers collapse. Sixty-six human beings dead.

Attica State Correction Facility. Prison riot. Forty-two human beings dead.

Ulster. Londonderry. Bogside. British paratroopers open fire. Thirteen people dead.

England. Aldershot. Bomb attack on barracks. Seven human beings dead.

Israel. Tel Aviv. Lod International Airport. Japanese Red Army attack. Twenty-five human beings dead.

Italy. Alitalia DC8 crashes into hill. One hundred and fifteen human beings dead.

Japan. Department store fire. One hundred and eighteen human beings dead.

England. Staines. BEA Trident crash. One hundred and eighteen humans dead.

Canada. Montreal. Nightclub bomb attack. Twenty-two human beings dead.

USA. California. Private plane crash into ice-cream parlour. Twenty-two human beings dead.

Mexico. Train crash. One hundred and forty-seven human beings dead.

Moscow. Plane crash. One hundred and seventy human beings dead.

Canary Islands. Plane crash. One hundred and fifty-five human beings dead.

Nicaragua. Managua. Christmas Day 1972. Earthquake. Ten thousand human beings dead.

Sinai. Libyan Boeing 727. Israeli fighter attack. Seventy-four human beings dead.

France. Two Spanish planes collide. Sixty-eight human beings dead.

Switzerland. Basle. Plane crash. One hundred and five human beings dead.

Isle of Man. Douglas. Funland fire. Fifty human beings dead.

Chile. Military coup. Two thousand human beings dead.

Mexico. Earthquake. Five hundred human beings dead.

Spain. Floods. Five hundred human beings dead.

Ethiopia. November 1973. Famine. Thousands and thousands and thousands of human beings dead.

"Jesus wept!" exclaimed Victor, smacking the breakfast table and making the breakfast things jump. "Just how much more of this shit is a person supposed to take?"

"What's bugging you?" demanded Suzie.

Victor stood up and threw his Guardian down.

"I've just about had it with this godforsaken planet."

He wagged an angry finger and marched out of the house and slammed the door as he went.

Baby Jane grinned through her Weetabix and spoke:

"Daddy's bonkers."

"Hmmmm," said Suzie.

London. Primrose Hill. Lorenzo's Delicatessen. One human being dead.

Millions of dead human beings had marched through Victor's frequently fevered brain, marched off endless newspaper pages and television screens. But Lorenzo was the first dead human being he had encountered in the flesh – and he found the reality banal.

He found himself thinking: "This is death?"

He found himself strangely underwhelmed.

Clearly, Lorenzo had staggered about quite a bit while "avvinisartattack" – and had caused some chaos in the process. He was sprawled in the aftermath of an avalanche of Panettone boxes, Grissini packets, broken glass and pasta: fettuccine, macaroni, pappardelle, linguine, rigatoni, rigor mortis.

An extra virgin olive oil slick eradicated friction underfoot. Victor slipped, went flying, landed with a wallop on the floor and found himself nose to nose with Lorenzo's cadaver.

Oh death, where is thy sting-a-ling-a-ling?
Oh grave, thy mystery?
The bells of hell go ting-a-ling-a-ling,
For you, but not for me.

Sung by some distant chorus of disembodied troops, this lunatic ditty popped, unbidden, into his head.

Were they referring to him or to his erstwhile employer? Victor did not believe in hell. In Victor's book, hell was a conceit, conceived by creeps for the coercion of cretins. To paraphrase the son of Christopher Wren: "Si infernum requiris, circumspice." If you want a hell, look about you.

With circumspect intent, Victor peered into the late Lorenzo Zerbi's vacant eyes.

He started to speak. He was about to say something along the lines of: "My friend, you're well out of it." But his voice sounded unspeakably strange, redundant in the room, so he held his tongue.

After the funeral, Lorenzo's widow, Marcella Zerbi, announced her intention to sella da business and return to Lucca.

Victor told Suzie it looked as though he would soon be out of a job. Suzie told George.

In the United Kingdom, over the fifteen years 1955 to 1970, the rate of inflation in the price of modern existing houses averaged five per cent per annum: somewhat faster than the rise in the cost of living. After 1970, there was a great surge in house prices: between December 1970 and December 1972 the average rise was no less than a remarkable thirty per cent per annum.

His academic career may have been a turkey, but when it came to the buying and selling of bricks and mortar, George was in the scholarship class.

Never mind thirty per cent per annum. In his first four years of business as a property developer, George, with Suzie by his side, refurbishing his canny buys, doubled his money, on an average, every six months.

It was a game. A secret game. He never spent a penny on himself. His only indulgence was a second-hand car, albeit a classic cream MGA with red leather upholstery, but that only cost five hundred pounds. He had no office. He had no fixed abode. He lived out of a suitcase. When Suzie did a property up, George moved in. When he sold it, he moved out, and onto the next.

When he became a millionaire, he kept it to himself. Suzie knew that George was doing pretty well. Hell's bells, at the beginning of 1974 he upped her pay to three hundred pounds a week, a lot, when you consider that Lorenzo had been paying Victor thirty-five pounds a week. But Suzie only knew about the houses on which she was working. She had no idea quite to what an extent George was raking it in. Even his accountants did not know. He had three accountants, none of whom knew of the others' existence, and four bank accounts, with four different banks, none of which was Barclays, and he took great pleasure in making sure that his right hand had no notion what his left hand was doing.

Frequently, of course, when his right hand was leafing through, say, a Barnard Marcus auction catalogue, his left hand would stray into his Y-fronts and, well, masturbation, if you'll pardon the expression, would occur. This is not to say that George found property particulars erotic. Quite the reverse in fact. But it is hard to keep a healthy penis down, especially one as underemployed as George's. And what with his right hand not knowing what his left hand was doing, and his natural bent for compartmentalisation, he would find himself reading with one part of his brain that a bedroom was eighteen feet eleven inches by thirteen feet seven inches, and wondering whether it could be subdivided into two, while another part of his brain, taking advantage of the situation, in collusion with his penis, would imagine that a bedroom was a place where sex occurs – and sometimes, God forgive him, there would sneak into his mind the image of Suzie and the ejaculating Glaswegian structural engineer.

It happened in 1973, when he was en route in the MGA

from Battersea to Wimbledon to view a house that was coming up for auction in two weeks time in May.

The night before, alone as ever, George had dined on a dubious take-away king prawn biryani, the consequences of which were ..... well, the word rhymes with dire rear, is almost impossible to spell without recourse to a dictionary, and we need not dwell upon it. Suffice it to say that the world fell out of his bottom.

Come the morning, George felt about two stone lighter, but otherwise intact, albeit somewhat shaky. He climbed into the car and set off in the direction of SW19.

At the bottom of West Hill, a band of die-hard biryani microbes mounted another attack. Thinking quickly, George hung a left and a right and a left again into Sispara Gardens, where he pulled up in front of a house he had acquired in January (on the day the Vietnam War came to a close).

There was Suzie's yellow Fiat parked outside, but George was in no state to observe it.

Grimacing, with buttocks clenched, he extricated himself from his car, minced absurdly up the garden path and, hopping from foot to foot, fumbled for the front door key, which was one of many on a bunch which he located in his pocket.

Into the lock with the key. Turn it. Stumble through the door. Quick! Along the passage, into the downstairs cloakroom. Oh no! The sanitary ware was there – but unconnected. Oh my God, hurry up. He beetled up the stairs, clenching for all he was worth, aiming for the master bedroom with its en-suite bathroom beyond.

Up the stairs, across the landing, the master bedroom door, seize the knob, turn it, open the door and – Good Grief!

Tableau!

Erotic tableau!!

Unbelievably erotic tableau!!!

Suzie and the gasping Glaswegian structural engineer.

At the sight of George in the door, Suzie sat back on her heels.

Too far gone to care, Mackenzie cried: "Dinna stop! Dinna stop!"

"Great timing, Porge," said Suzie.

"Oh Christ!" Mackenzie moaned.

George gawped, as the structural engineer's gravity-defying member bobbed, bounced, lurched and shot a massive ejaculatory wad, which sailed over Suzie's head and landed on the brand new sky-blue deep-pile broadloom carpet.

Beetroot red and speechless, George, desperate to retreat, was also desperate to advance. The chaos in his colon drove him on, across the compromised carpet and into the en suite bathroom, where, thank God, the plumbing was complete. He slammed the door, dropped his pants and made it onto the antique Shanks, which Suzie had located at the bottom of the Portobello Road, just in time. He leaned forward, put his elbows on his knees, his head in his hands, and surrendered, with a whimper, to his malodorous affliction.

When he came out of the bathroom, the structural engineer was gone. Suzie was on her hands and knees, scrubbing at his far-flung passionate deposit, while heaving with helpless laughter.

"What's so funny?"

"God, Porge," she giggled. "The look on your face. You should have seen it. Priceless!"

George was utterly flummoxed by his sister's apparent lack of shame.

"Now, Porge, I mean, George, now listen," said Suzie, "I'm only going to say this once. It's my life. It's the only one I've got. And I'll do what I want with it. OK?"

George considered his sister, considered the stain and said: "Will it come out?"

"If it doesn't, I'll pay for it."

"Make bloody Mackenzie pay for it." He looked at his watch. "I have to go. I'm late for an appointment."

He headed for the door.

"George?"

"What?"

"You wouldn't tell Victor, would you?"

"Tell Victor what?"

"Thanks, Porge," said Suzie. "I'm sorry, by the way."

"Well, that's a first."

"How do you mean?"

"I don't think I've ever heard you say sorry to anyone before. Certainly not to me."

"Well, I am sorry. I'm sorry if I embarrassed you."

"It doesn't matter," said George. "I'll see you later."

He left, with yet another secret stashed away underneath his belt.

Suzie went shopping – first to Comyn Ching for door furniture: knobs, escutcheons, spindles, finger-plates, rising hinges, levers, latches, bolts. Then on the Peter Jones to order up some blinds.

Suzie's job for George involved shopping. Serious shopping. Day in, day out. Shopping for things and shopping for people – plumbers, plasterers, painters, electricians, structural engineers.

At school, she had been taught that the function of the Holy Spirit was to bring order out of chaos. Now she found that shopping kept chaos at bay. She whipped it into shape with her George Perry No.2 Business Account credit card.

At half past two, she re-rendez-vous-ed with Malcolm Mackenzie in a house in Maple Close, in Clapham Park. There was structural engineering work to be done. There was a wall that needed to come down. And then there was the question of the other unfinished business. Having whipped chaos into shape at Peter Jones and Comyn Ching, there remained the chaos in her blood, which could only be kept at bay, in Suzie's mind, by quivering encounters with men for whom, when all was said and done, she did not give a damn.

Apart from which, sex, at home, was out, in the wake of Suzie's ultimatum on the subject of a second child.

"It's clear to me," she said, "that you don't love me."

"Of course I love you," said Victor. "Of course I want you. I'm desperate for you. But I simply do not want a second child."

"What? Never?"

"Did I say never? I'm talking about now. Come on, Suzie, go back on the pill. I want to make love to you."

"I want to make love to you too, Victor. And I want another baby."

"What do you want another baby **for**? What's wrong with the one you've got?"

"Don't you love her?"

"You know I do. What's that got to do with it?"

"What's so terrible about having another baby?"

"Well, for one thing," said Victor, "apart from anything else, we're living on a grossly over-populated planet. Half the people are grossly undernourished, starving to death in fact, and you want to produce yet another mouth to feed. It's grossly irresponsible."

"We can afford it."

"You can afford it."

"What's mine is yours, Victor. You know that."

"Listen," said Victor, huffing and puffing, "I'm not talking about money here. How dare you bring the subject down to money? It's disgraceful. I'm talking about the fucking future of the fucking human race here. And you want to talk about money? It's obscene."

"Bullshit," said Suzie.

"It's not bullshit."

"It is," she countered crossly. "And you know it."

She turned her back on him. Shoulder blades by Bernini. Spine by Michelangelo. Strong, slim, alluring to the seventeenth degree. She shut her eyes, relaxed and went to sleep. How could she go to sleep like that, in the wake of such a painful row? What kind of a game was she playing? It did not occur to Victor that, after a hard day's work, the girl was simply exhausted.

Victor pulled on his dressing-gown, went downstairs and stared at a blank sheet of paper.

Absurdly, both of them were lying.

Victor was scared. He was scared the baby would be born with something wrong. It was scary enough waiting for Jane to make an appearance. Wasn't a second one pushing their luck? He was scared the second one would be a boy, and then they would have to get into that whole circumcision thing again. He was scared that fatherhood had already seriously compromised his literary powers. Who was it who had once said that art could not endure a perambulator parked in the passage? He was scared that a second child would put the kybosh once and for all on his Pulitzer-prize-winning chances. And he was scared, because he did not seem to be able to make any money, and whatever Suzie told him, and whatever he told himself, over and over and over again, to the effect that the money was neither here nor there, and he was above all that – he wasn't. In so far as Victor could barely go shopping at all, chaos nipped incessantly at his heels and undermined his peace of mind. And right deep down, to his chagrin, to his shame, he felt inadequate – as a husband and, more particularly, as a father. And if he felt inadequate with one child, how much more inadequate would he feel with two?

And Suzie was lying, because, in fact, she had not stopped taking the pill. She wanted a second child. And she wanted it with Victor, not with some plumber or some painter or some structural engineer. But she wanted it with Victor's full and willing co-operation. And until such time as he changed his mind, Suzie saw no harm in letting him believe that there would be no copulation without procreation in their bed.

So, when Lorenzo died, then, it would be fair to say that their marriage was in some need of attention. And it occurred to Suzie that if she bought the deli from Mrs Zerbi and gave it to Victor, this might go some way towards redressing the balance in their life. With this end in mind, she spoke to George and asked him if he would buy the deli for her.

"I don't want to buy a deli," said George.

"No, I want you to buy it for me, on my behalf, with my money."

"What money?"

"The money I've been saving. Come on, George. I need you to do all the negotiating and stuff. You know you're bloody good at it."

George looked into the matter and discovered, in the course of his researches, that, in 1971, Lorenzo had applied for planning permission to turn the delicatessen into a restaurant, and that he had acquired a full justice's on-licence, subject to the planning permission being given, and that the planning permission had indeed been granted.

When George approached the understandably distraught Mrs Zerbi, he further discovered that these permissions were not reflected in the delicatessen's asking price, for the simple reason that the grieving widow knew nothing about them, her husband never having told her. Lorenzo, having failed to raise sufficient cash to realise his ambition of turning the deli into a trattoria, had kept his dream to himself.

A restaurant lease is far more valuable than a shop lease. Stifling his excitement, George made an offer, on his own behalf, and clinched the deal.

Then he called Suzie and asked her what she wanted to hear first: the good news or the bad news?

"The bad news."

"She's already sold it to someone else."

"Damn," said Suzie. "And the good news?"

"I've managed to buy all the stock and equipment off the new owners for a very keen price."

"Oh brilliant," said Suzie, "what am I supposed to do with that?"

"You know the wool shop, opposite the garage, in the Lower Richmond Road?"

"What about it?"

"It's just closed down."

"Do you think we could get it?"

"I've already spoken to the new landlord, and he's prepared to offer you extremely advantageous terms."

"Brilliant," said Suzie. "Well done, George."

Somehow or other, George neglected to mention that the building belonged to him, and that he was the landlord in question. And he could not see that it was anybody else's business but his own that, one month later, he sold on the deli in Primrose Hill to M.P.M., the voracious restaurant chain, at a profit so enormous it left him short of breath and laughing for a week.

20

JANE'S FOOD SHOP

There was much flaring of the nostrils, flexing of the pecs and general all-round exercising of the ego, when Suzie told Victor that she had bought him a delicatessen in the Lower Richmond Road.

"You could've told me."

"I'm telling you now."

"You could've consulted me."

"Youd've said No."

"Not necessarily."

She laughed: "You're like the Frenchman with the fish."

He was indignant: "What Frenchman?"

"You know – his wife bought two fish for supper, one big, one small, and she gave him the small fish and kept the big one for herself. So he said: 'If I'd been doing the cooking, I'd have given you the big fish, and I'd have given myself the small fish.' To which she replies: 'Well, that's what you've got. What are you complaining about?'"

"I'm not complaining, I'm ….."

"You're huffing and puffing."

"A person's entitled to huff and puff when he's not consulted."

Having huffed and puffed for a couple of days, however, Victor came round.

So it was charity. So what? Is charity so terrible? Charity's a two-way thing. For a person to be charitable, another person has to be charitable enough to accept that person's charity. To turn down Suzie's gift would be uncharitable.

He had to admit to himself that, had he been consulted, he would have said no to the plan. He would have thought: it's all very well being a great unknown writer and working in somebody else's delicatessen, because you can still put "Writer" down as your description in your passport, so to speak. But when the delicatessen is actually yours, don't you then become a "Delicatessen Owner" and sort of cease to be a "Writer" any more?

Well, hadn't he sort of ceased to be a writer? What was he writing? He wasn't actually writing anything at all, because, in fact, he could not think of anything to write.

"You need a break from writing," Suzie said. "You need a break from banging your head against a brick wall. Give yourself a break. Join the real world."

He had to admit, in the end, that she had a point. A break would be sweet. Failing to do anything, when you're trying to do something, is exhausting. It would be a relief, for five minutes, not even to try. He would make a positive decision to do nothing. And anyway, when all was said and done, he could always put it down to research.

"I'll do it for Jane," he said, still wriggling on the hook of his own self-image.

"Well, good for you," said Suzie.

"In fact," he went on, warming to his role as the selfless, all-sacrificing father, "I think it would be an altogether more …….. felicitous arrangement, if we put the business in her name."

"Would that make you happy?"

"It would."

"Then that's what we'll do."

And that is what they did. They put the delicatessen in their daughter's name, and they called it: Victor's Daughter's Deli? Bit of a mouthful. Delice de Putney? Do me a favour. The Lower

Richmond Road Delicatessen? Too boring. Cornucopia? Too pretentious. Dunstarvin'? Be serious. How about Jane's Food Shop? Well, why not? I like it. They both liked it. Jennifer liked it, and so did Mary Poppins. And that is, then, what it was called: Jane's Food Shop.

From Number Nine to Jane's Food Shop was a fifteen minute walk, up Castelnau, across the Common, and down the Lower Richmond Road.

Victor embraced his new responsibilities with vigour. Out from under the thrall of literature's tyrannical muse, he was free to focus his formidable powers of concentration on something he was actually very good at. He was off at half past six, never back before nine, seemingly seven days a week.

Victor's father used to say: "Greengrocery? It's a mug's game. You want to sell a potato? First, peel it. Boil it. Mix with it some mayonnaise. Snip a chive. Make a potato salad. Now you've got something you can sell."

But you had to make that potato salad yourself. It was no good buying someone else's added value. You had to add the value yourself.

"Who knows how to make mayonnaise?"

"I do," said Jennifer.

"Good," said Victor, "you're in charge of mayonnaise. How about sausage rolls?"

"I can make sausage rolls," said Mary Poppins.

"What about me?" asked Jane, who was not such a baby any more. She was six, rather solemn, (in the Porge mode), somewhat chunky, with shiny straight black hair and eyes like lychee stones.

"What can you make, sweetheart?"

"Biscuits."

"Right, you're in charge of biscuits. You can be the Cookie Queen."

The Cookie Queen went into action, in the kitchen of Number Nine, every afternoon after school.

Putting the delicatessen into her name had been an unconscious stroke of genius. He would never have got them all at it, if it had simply been his. Under the circumstances, though, they could hardly refuse.

Oh yes, Victor had them all at it, boiling hams, baking cakes, raising pies, roasting chickens, simmering jams, steaming puddings, peeling and chopping and mixing and rolling and generally having a really rather wonderful time.

Mary Poppins' Sausage Rolls sold like hot cakes. Grandma Perry's Hot Cakes sold like Mary Poppins' Sausage Rolls. And Jane fell behind in her homework, so great was the demand for her Jumbo Gingerbread Elephants and Miniature Macaroons.

In the midst of all this pungent activity, Victor underwent a change of heart. Strangely, broodiness stole upon him. He began to have dynastic longings. Never mind the baby carriage in the hallway, what about Tolstoy? How many children did Tolstoy have? Hundreds. And did they interfere with his output, or what? I mean, how productive was Tolstoy? Exactly.

Victor looked upon his daughter with new eyes. There was never any question but that he had loved the little tyke from the moment she was born. And any suggestion that he resented her presence was hotly refuted. It was only at the moment, though, that he actually did stop resenting her presence, that he finally realised quite how much he had always resented her presence up to that point.

It was a Saturday. Suzie picked Jane up from ballet and dropped her off at the Food Shop. Jane was still wearing her tutu, a frothy pink confection. A silver plastic crown was perched on top of her head, and she carried a bedraggled home-made magic wand.

"Don't you think she'd be better off at home with Mary Poppins?"

"Victor, she's been looking forward to helping you all week."

"Well, she's not properly dressed."

"She's perfectly dressed. She's the Cookie Queen."

"And if the Cookie Queen catches a cold and gets a temperature, I suppose that doesn't matter?"

"Oh, for goodness sake, Victor, stop being so anally retentive. I'll pick her up at three. Bye bye, Pudding."

"I'm not a pudding," said Jane. "I'm the Cookie Queen."

Suzie bowed low to the diminutive monarch and buzzed off to a rendez-vous in Pimlico which hummed with erotic potential.

Victor went about his business. Customers came and went. Singing gently to herself, while counting packets of flageolets, Jane was no trouble at all, but in some secret place, which Victor would not recognise, he resented her presence nonetheless.

Enter Mr and Mrs Conrad Dwick of Roehampton. They pulled up outside in a beige and brown Rolls Royce.

"Good morning," said Victor, with a sinking heart, "what can I get you?"

"Conrad," said Mrs Dwick, prodding her husband.

Mr Dwick took a deep and long-suffering breath, hardened his hangdog features as far as was in his power, thrust out all his chins and said: "Are you the owner of this establishment?"

"I am," Victor confessed.

"My wife bought some yoghurt from you and it was mouldy. What do you intend doing about it?"

"Oh dear," said Victor, amiably. "May I have a look?"

"No you may not. It's gone down the waste disposal unit. It stank."

"And when did you open it?"

"I opened it this morning," Mrs Dwick intervened, "and it was covered with green mould."

Mrs Dwick was the kind of customer you do not forget in a hurry, much as you might like to.

"I'm sorry, I don't know your name," said Victor, addressing the husband, as the lesser of two evils.

"Dwick," said the man.

"Mr Dwick," said Victor, "your wife bought that yoghurt last Friday. That's over a week ago. I remember her very well. She bought one ounce of gruyère, three ounces of ham, six black olives – and the yoghurt." Victor, still in vaguely conciliatory mode, neglected to mention that the stupid woman had spent three quarters of an hour negotiating these tiresome purchases.

"So you don't dispute it?" said Dwick.

Victor came out from behind his counter, crossed to the chill cabinet and removed from it one pot of yoghurt.

A self-satisfied smile further distorted Mrs Dwick's far from prepossessing features. She thought she was about to get a pot of yoghurt for free.

"Mrs Dwick, this is what you bought, isn't it?"

"Yes, it is," agreed la Dwick.

"Mrs Dwick, can you read?"

"What do you mean by that?"

"Now, look here," her husband blustered.

"Look," said Victor, holding up the pot to her startled face, "in black and white: 'To be consumed within four days of purchase.'"

"Are you trying to suggest that that yoghurt wasn't mouldy when I bought it?"

"Of course it wasn't mouldy when you bought it. It went mouldy in your fridge, if you kept it in a fridge."

"Are you calling my wife a liar?"

"Am I calling your wife a liar? I'm calling her bluff. I've been in this business since I was seven years old. This is a typical two-tone Rolls Royce scam. What is it about you two-tone Rolls-Royce people? Why are you always more trouble than anyone else?"

"I'm not staying here to be insulted," said Mrs Dwick.

"Please don't," said Victor.

"You haven't heard the last of this," said Mr Dwick.

"You deserve to go bust," Mrs Dwick opined, then she rummaged about in her limited vocabulary for a suitable aspersion and added: "You .... lout."

At this point in the conversation, Jane, the Cookie Queen, marched up to the woman, prodded her in the stomach with her wand and said:

"Don't you speak to my daddy like that, you pooey pig-bum, or I'll chop off your head."

Victor thought his heart would explode with mirth and pride.

"What did you call me?" hissed Mrs Dwick, assuming a mien so Cruella-de-Ville-ish, brave little Jane backed off in alarm.

"You heard," said Victor. "You're a pooey pig-bum and you better watch out or she'll chop off your head."

"Come on, Conrad, we're going. This'll teach me not to shop at Harrods."

Conrad Dwick pulled himself up to his full lack of height and strutted off after his wife. He turned at the door for a parting shot.

"We shall tell all our friends," he said.

"You have friends?" Victor was amazed.

Exit the Dwicks.

And enter a new-found fondness for this infant prodigy of his. The kid was on his team. The kid was brilliant, inspirational. "Pooey pig-bum." Was that an insult, or what?"

And exit Victor's unacknowledged resentment of the little girl, and as it faded away, he recognised it for what it had been and felt ashamed of himself.

And enter the following radical thought: whereas with secret meanness he had hitherto considered himself to be overladen in the offspring department to the tune of one, he now began to wonder whether one was anywhere near enough. Here he had been, all this time, blaming his only child for hindering his literary output, when all along, perhaps, he should have been producing far more children. Think Tolstoy.

Imagine Suzie's surprise, therefore, when Victor came to bed that night in priapic mood, snuggled in and snuggled up and whispered in her ear:

"OK. You're on. Let's have another one."

Thinking quickly, Suzie lied: "I have my period."

"Excuse me," Victor grinned, "who else's period should you be having?"

"Very funny, Victor. You've changed your tune. Has something happened to the population of the planet I don't know about?"

"I have decided that what we need is more people like Jane to counteract the Dwicks of this world."

"Who are the Dwicks?"

"Pooey pig-bums."

"She didn't!" Suzie exclaimed, when Victor filled her in.

"She certainly did."

"Well, good for her."

They enjoyed a companionable giggle and a cuddle, which was chaste, then Victor fell asleep, and Suzie fell to wondering whether or not she should come off the pill.

No.

There were things that she wanted to do, people she wanted to screw. Pregnancy would not be convenient right now.

Suzie was quite without guilt when it came to her extramarital sexual activities. As far as she was concerned, she had one life, one body, one chance, and what she did with it in her own time was nobody's business but her own. She had no compunction about lying to Victor, should the occasion arise. Nor did she feel the slightest compunction to "tell him the truth". The truth was that Suzie did not feel he needed to know. And what is truth? And, more to the point, what is honesty? As far as Suzie was concerned, it was not the cant and selfishness which describes itself as honesty and makes a fetish out of spilling the beans come hell or high water.

She climbed out of bed, went into the bathroom, inspected her face in the mirror, attacked a blackhead with a satisfying squish, and pondered:

"The truth is, if I am honest with myself, that I like my life the way it is. I like being married to Victor, and I like fucking around – and it doesn't worry Victor, coz Victor don't know. On the other hand, if I did tell Victor, he might be terribly upset. So why cause him pain? Or even, knowing how perverse he is, Victor might not be upset at all, in which case, I have to admit, I think that I'd be upset. In fact, I know I'd be upset. So why cause myself pain? The truth is that, before anything else, you have to be honest with yourself, and if you're truly honest with yourself, and can see yourself for what you are, the way forward will become clear." She frowned. "Er, so what am I?" Then she smiled.

"I'm me," she said, to her reflection over the sink – and went back to bed.

Suzie stayed on the pill, then, while allowing Victor fondly to imagine that she was off it. The consequence of this was that, over the following months, millions and millions of Victor's sperms went off on a wild goose chase.

21

BRICKS & MORTAR

In the long hot summer of 1976, Suzie developed a pain in her upper abdomen, on the left-hand side.

"Are you alright, darling?" Jennifer anxiously enquired, over lunch at San Frediano's, in the Fulham Road.

"I'm fine. I'm fine," said Suzie.

"You're nor pregnant?" Jennifer whispered, as if anyone could hear her over San Fred's din.

"No, I'm not. It's just a bit of indigestion."

Suzie gave up on her gnocchi, rustled up a bright smile and addressed herself to the point of this mother and daughter outing.

"Now look, Mum, I've been thinking ……."

How exactly was she going to put this?

"Is something the matter?" asked her mother, gently.

"No, no, nothing at all. It's just that, the thing is, I've been thinking about the house ……"

"What house?"

"Number Nine – and it occurred to me that it's a very big house and, if we didn't live there, Victor and Jane and me, you'd probably have moved out a long time ago by now."

"Susan, if I didn't want you to live there, you'd be the first to know. You know me. I'm not backward in coming forward. The fact of the matter is that the present arrangements suit me very well. I've grown quite used to Victor. And dear little Jane, well, she keeps me young. I'd miss her desperately, if you went. So you see, you don't need to worry about me. I'm very happy with things as they are."

"Well, I'm not. I want a house of my own."

"Oh dear, Susan, I am sorry. I hope you don't think for a minute that I was in any way implying .... I mean, that I was trying to put pressure on you not to go. Of course, you must have a house of your own. Can't you make George find one for you?"

"I'm perfectly capable of finding a house for myself. No, the problem is that Victor won't wear it."

"Victor won't wear what?" wondered Jennifer. Had she missed something? How had they slipped into clothing?

"He doesn't want to move."

"Oh? Why not?"

"Well, he rambles on about Jane and the close bond she has with Mary Poppins, and the close bond she has with you, and he doesn't want to unsettle her. And then it's very convenient for work, and he loves the house, and he's a typical bloody Taurean, and he doesn't want to move. But the real problem is ...."

Suzie paused, experienced the pain in her abdomen, on the left hand side, sipped at her wine.

"Money?" Jennifer prompted.

"In a nutshell. Yes. He couldn't afford a house anywhere near as nice as Number Nine, so he kids himself he doesn't want to move."

"I see."

"And the thing is, thanks to dear old George, I could afford a very nice house, but I don't think I'd ever get Victor to agree to let me buy it."

"You bought the food shop."

"That was different – and it wasn't exactly easy getting him to agree to that – but what I was thinking was: why don't I buy Number Nine?"

"Whatever for?"

In the midst of the restaurant's clatter and chatter, Suzie laid her cards on the table. She wanted to buy Number Nine. This would be a private deal between her and her mother. Her mother would have complete security of tenure, as would Mary Poppins. Ostensibly, it would still be Jennifer's house. But Jennifer would have the money from the house in her bank account, to do with as she pleased. So, if for any reason, she wanted to up sticks and go, to somewhere smaller, to somewhere more private, to live in Monaco or Timbuctoo or up the road or wherever, she would have the wherewithal so to do, should she be so inclined. And, should she be so inclined, she would not have the worry about what Victor and Jane and she would do for somewhere to live. And, as far as Suzie was concerned, owning the house would fulfil a fundamental need. It would give her a stability she felt was lacking in her life. It would …….. Suzie ground to a halt. Why exactly was it that she found the notion of owning Number Nine so appealing?

"But Susan," objected her mother, "supposing that you and Victor do decide, at some later stage, that you want to live on your own after all, that you want to move, you won't be able to do it. All your capital will be tied up."

"I can always sell it to George."

"I wouldn't sell it to George. He'd chop it up into flats, like they did to the Foster-Wilsons', and ruin it."

"I've already made a deal with him. He's promised never to do that, certainly for as long as you and Mary Poppins are …….."

"Alive?"

"Want to live there."

"Hmmm. You've discussed this with George?"

"George is very good on bricks and mortar, and he's exceedingly discreet."

"You both are. You like your little secrets. You take after your father. And how much does George think that my bricks and mortar are worth?"

"Well, George's ideas on value all depend on whether he's buying or selling. I think the fairest thing would be to get three separate independent valuations and take the middle price."

"Tell me, Susan," Jennifer began, in the manner of one about to move into another and altogether more sensitive area, "do you ever talk to George?"

"I talk to him all the time."

"No, I mean, really talk to him."

"About what?"

"Well, you know, girl-friends, sex, that sort of thing."

"No, I don't. He's not that sort of person."

"He's never had a girl-friend, has he?"

"He's far too busy playing Monopoly and making money."

"You don't think he's …….. gay?"

"Who? George? Gay?" This was an interesting thought. "I wouldn't have thought so. I mean, he's so straight, isn't he? He's so conventional."

"I don't think he's conventional at all," said George's mother. "I think he's positively odd."

Suzie laughed.

"Well, don't you think he's odd?"

Suzie considered for a moment, then said:

"I don't think he's all that much odder than anybody else."

At which point, the odd one in question entered the restaurant and wended his way up to the table with an admittedly somewhat demented twinkle in his eye.

"Hello, George," said Jennifer. "This is a nice surprise."

"Guess what," said George. "I've just bought a house."

"So what else is new?" said Suzie.

"No, I mean, a house for myself, not to sell, for myself. This one's going to be my home."

"Where is it?" asked Suzie.

"Holland Park. It's fantastic. I want you to do it up for me. Carte blanche. You'll love it."

Suzie did her level best to be enthusiastic, but Jennifer could see that she was cut to the quick, and determined then and there to go along with her plan and let her buy Number Nine.

Suzie attempted to pay the bill, but Jennifer insisted it was her treat. Then Jennifer went off in a taxi to Peter Jones with a view to buying Jane a nice new summer frock, while George and Suzie went next door into Piero de Monzi's.

George, needing a suit for Tom's forthcoming wedding, had asked Suzie to help him pick one out. And Suzie had insisted that Piero's was the place for him to go.

Dressing George up in Cerrutti suits was fun, but she could not help wishing that it was Victor she was with. Victor, though, would never, even if he was rich, have paid that kind of money for a suit. He would have felt uncomfortable in it, thinking of dead Ethiopian babies, whose lives might have been saved, had he spent the money on them, had not vanity intervened. Considerations of this kind were outside George's ken. He only objected to paying, because he was mean, which only made Suzie more determined to make him spend a lot.

They emerged from Piero's, laden with shopping, into the afternoon heat, while, round the world, people were dropping, without any clothes, nor shoes on their feet.

George had traded in the MGA for an irresistible dove-grey drop-head Mercedes. They chucked the carrier bags in the back and motored over to Holland Park to look at the house.

"My God, it's vast," Suzie gasped. "How much did it cost?"

"It was a very good buy. Do you like it?"

"It's incredible. How many rooms?"

"About twenty – give or take a bog."

"George, what do you want with twenty rooms?"

"Well, living-room, drawing-room, dining-room, breakfast-room, kitchen, library ......"

"You can't read."

"Up yours. Television room. Jigsaw-puzzle-and-Scrabble room. Ping-pong room. My office. Secretary's office. Your studio. Guest suite ....."

"Hold on a minute. My studio?"

"I thought you ought to have a space of your own in the business part of the house. Guest suite: bedroom, bathroom, dressing-room. Spare room, spare bathroom. Staff quarters."

"What staff?"

"I thought I might get a couple. So they'll need a bedroom, bathroom, sitting-room and kitchen of their own."

"What? No chauffeur?"

"I don't think there's any more space for a chauffeur. I've run out of rooms. I mean, don't forget, I'm planning to live here as well."

She'd never seen George so happy. He was hopping from one foot to the other and rubbing his hands together with glee, as he showed her round his ambassadorial abode.

That night, when she was brushing her teeth, blood appeared in the Colgate foam. Suzie rinsed out her mouth and inspected her teeth. Inspecting her teeth, she caught a glimpse of the skull within her skin. Arguably, teeth are the skeleton's only visible part. When the flesh falls away, the teeth remain, embedded in the bone. Morbid thoughts. She banished them. She prodded her gums. It was her gums which were bleeding. Clearly, she had been wielding her toothbrush with an excess of vigour.

Victor refused to come to the wedding, of Tom to Veronica Hudson, a girl whom Tom had met over a glass-topped coffee table, striped with lines of cocaine, at a party in the New King's Road. She had a ten bob note up her nose. In Tom's book, Ronnie, as Veronica was known, was cool.

"Who's going to look after the shop, if I come?" was Victor's official line.

"You can close up the shop for one day," protested Suzie.

"On a Saturday? Are you crazy? Saturday's the busiest day of the week."

"So what? This is an important family outing, and I'd like you to come."

"Listen, the food shop may be a stupid little side-line to you. But it's my business, and I take it seriously."

"Well, actually, it's Jane's business, isn't it? And she's going to be a bridesmaid and I think you should be there to see her do her stuff."

This was a potent argument, but Victor dug in his heels. He was damned if he would close up the shop for that wastrel drug addict, Tom.

The day of the wedding dawned. Dennis Howell, the newly appointed Minister for Drought, groaned. The black cloud over Victor's head was the only cloud in the otherwise endless blazing blue sky. He set off for the Food Shop with a scowl, and woe betide the customer who dared to give him lip.

In the bathroom, getting ready, Suzie inspected her limbs. Mysterious bruises had appeared on her arms and legs. Where the fuck had they come from? She had been planning to wear a sleeveless dress, quite short, with no tights. It was far too hot for tights. Instead, she chose a trouser suit, in linen, which covered up the mysterious bruises.

"You look lovely," Jennifer said, when Suzie came downstairs.

"Thank you. So do you. Where's Jane?"

"Helping Mary Poppins with her stays."

Suzie perched herself on the edge of a chair, and fanned her face with her floppy hat.

"Darling," said Jennifer, "if I did agree to let you buy the house, you wouldn't want to 'do it up', would you?"

Suzie smiled and shook her golden head.

"No. I like the house as it is. Well, maybe our bathroom could do with a little attention."

"Fair enough. But otherwise you'd be content to leave things as they are?"

"Absolutely. It's perfect. It's our home. I love it."

Jennifer smiled.

"Well then," she said, "in that case, I think that you and I can do business."

"Oh Mum, thank you. I can't tell you how much it means to me. I don't really know why, but it does."

"Well, good," said Jennifer. "I'm pleased. I'll speak to Graham first thing on Monday morning."

(Graham Stanley – family solicitor.)

"Mummy! Mummy! Look at me! cried Jane, skipping into the room, in her bridesmaid dress. "Aren't I beautiful!"

"Utterly gorgeous."

For a moment there, the heatwave's warmth was nothing to the warmth she felt inside.

George came by and picked them up in the Mercedes. Suzie and Jennifer sat in the back with Jane inbetween them. Mary Poppins rode up front with George. The late Queen Mary never looked so grand.

"Actually," said Jane, "I think it's a very good thing that Daddy isn't coming."

"Oh really? Why's that?" asked Suzie.

"Well, there wouldn't be anywhere for him to sit. You see," she explained, with the wonderful pedantry of advanced youth, "there are five people in this car, and if Daddy came, there would be six, and there isn't any room for six, even though this car is very very big."

"He could sit on your lap," suggested George.

"Oh, Uncle George, don't be so silly."

"If your father had come," said Mary Poppins, turning round and peering at Jane, from under the brim of her hat, "you, my girl, would have had to go in the boot."

"No, I wouldn't. You'd have to go in the boot."

"Careful, Jane," Jennifer cautioned. "Don't be cheeky."

"Oh, grandma, I wouldn't really put Mary Poppins in the boot."

"I'd really put your father in the boot," said Suzie, with some feeling, "and I'd lock it and I'd throw away the key."

"Actually, Mummy, I think you're right. Daddy should go into the boot, because Daddy's got a spare tyre, and that's where spare tyres go – in the boot!"

Well, that put Victor in his place. They chuckled off into the melting haze, into the gasping countryside.

22

GRAVITY'S CLAW

It was a marriage made in cocaine heaven. The bride and groom ground their teeth through the service, sniffed as they made their eternal vows and, during the reception, made innumerable trips to the bathroom to powder (the inside of) their noses.

The reception occurred in a large marquee, erected in the garden of Ronnie's parents' rambling house, in Virginia Water.

Tom's father, Hugo Foster-Wilson, having suffered a stroke in 1975, was not present. He was in Miami, which was all for the best on the diplomatic front.

His mother was there, with her new husband, a widowed and retired high court judge, whose name was Rupert Harper-Wake, known as Half-Awake in his days on the bench.

"Well," said Tom, when he learned that his mother was about to change her name again and that his step-father-to-be was also double-barrelled, "at least she gets to keep her hyphen."

Caroline Harper-Wake, then, seemed to be very happy, very centred, if you'll pardon the expression, and assured. They were living in one of Oxford's grandest houses.

"Yes," she said to Jennifer, "life is very good."

Jennifer experienced a sensation, which, for a moment, she was at a loss to name. How long had it been since she felt a sensation like that? It was jealousy. It was most unpleasant. She quashed it.

"I'm very happy for you, Caroline."

"You will come down to stay?"

"That would be very nice."

George was commandeered by Ronnie's second cousin, a girl called Wendy Green. Wendy was as voluptuous as Ronnie was thin. She was a researcher at the BBC. On seeing the Mercedes, parked on the gravel outside, she immediately switched into research mode, and having ascertained that George was its right and lawful owner, made a bee-line for him. He did not stand a chance.

Jane latched onto Lupin, the Hudsons' English bull terrier. Jane would have dearly loved to own a dog. But Victor's heart was set against pets.

Of a sudden, Suzie felt weak. She made her excuses to Ronnie's mother's imbecilic aunt and went to find Mary Poppins, who was having conversation, at a corner table, with a dark-eyed handsome man.

The dark-eyed handsome man was Anton Cohen – Tom's friend, Anton, who went off to Edinburgh to read medicine.

"You remember Anton," Mary Poppins prompted.

"Of course I do," said Suzie, sitting down. "Excuse me, I think I'm going to faint."

"Is that a statement of fact or a figure of speech?"

"Figure of speech," lied Suzie. "It's the heat. I crave a cool, dark room."

She scrunched up her eyes, shook her face, stretched and blinked her faintness away. The pain in her abdomen on the left hand side, however, did not go away.

"This girl is ill," said Mary Poppins. "She's far too thin. She's far too pale. And she's ill. But will she see a doctor? Of course, she won't. She knows better."

"Give it a rest, Mary, there's a good girl."

"Anton's a doctor, you know."

"I know he is."

"Well," said Mary Poppins, standing up, "I'm going to get

myself some food."

"Jesus," said Suzie, "how subtle was that?"

"So, what are your symptoms?"

"Life in the second part of the twentieth century? Will that do you?"

"Listen, sorry. I had to ask. I was under orders."

"Mary thinks she knows us all better than we know ourselves. But she doesn't. I'm fine."

They sat for a moment or two in companionable silence, thinking this and that, knowing that they shared some kind of interconnected past, but the details – the climbing frame, sailing through the air on the day her father died, landing on Anton's castle made of sand, flattening it, breaking her bones – the details were lost in the good old mists of time.

"I'll tell you who isn't fine," Anton remarked, in a conversational way.

"Who?"

"Tom. I'm very worried about him."

"I wouldn't worry about Tom, if I were you."

"No? You don't find his cocaine consumption alarming?"

"What cocaine consumption?"

"Oh, come off it."

"It's none of my business."

"No?"

Anton fixed her with a squinty kind of smile. He really was a very handsome man.

"Listen," said Suzie. "Tom has always maintained that whatever a person does in the privacy of his own bloodstream is nobody else's business but his own – and I go along with that."

"Well, I don't. I think it's crap."

"Why?"

"Suzie, I'm a doctor. What do you expect me to say?"

"Are you a good doctor?"

"The best."

"Where do you practise?"

"Highgate."

He pulled out a wallet and handed her his card.

"Are you married?"

"No."

"Involved?"

"What is this? Twenty questions?"

Suzie laughed, as Mary Poppins returned to the table, bearing a plate of food.

Anton rose and excused himself. He needed ten minutes alone to work on his speech. He was Tom's best man.

"Mummy! Mummy! Mummy!"

In a state of high excitement, Jane beetled up to the table.

"What is it, darling?"

"You'll never guess what!"

"What?"

"Lupin's done a huge poo in Uncle George's car!"

"Oh God. What was Lupin doing in George's car?"

"Well, you see, I was driving her to India and she couldn't hold it in. It's incredibly smelly."

Suzie slipped Anton's card into her bag and went to investigate. They missed the speeches, cleaning up the mess.

"Now, Jane, whatever you do, don't tell George."

"Alright."

"Promise?"

"I promise. Mummy, can we have a dog?"

"You must be joking."

In the pet debate, Suzie had been sitting on the fence. Lupin's grim deposit pushed her firmly off it, into Victor's camp.

On the way home, Jennifer, Jane and Mary Poppins sat in the back – all three of them fell asleep.

"What's that smell?" asked George, wrinkling his nose.

"I can't smell anything," said Suzie.

"I can."

"Oh, that. That's just good old English country air."

"It smells like dogshit to me."

"Bullshit," Suzie replied, ambiguously.

George was unconvinced, but he had other things to occupy his mind. Somehow or other, he seemed to have ended up with a date, for the following week, with Wendy Green. She had kissed him goodbye, lightly on the lips and, in so doing, caused his toes to curl.

Considering her cleavage, as he drove along, he felt a strange constriction round his heart. Christine Keeler's cleavage, all those years ago, had worked a very similar effect. But Christine Keeler's cleavage, as far as George was concerned, was black and white and strictly two-dimensional... Wendy Green's cleavage, on the other hand, had featured in startling 3-D, was tanned, heaved quite a bit and was, what with the heatwave and everything, moist.

Beside her brother, Suzie sat, staring straight ahead, as insects hit the windscreen – and died.

She could lie with ease to anyone else. She found it unbearably hard to lie to herself. But still, she would not surrender herself to the truth.

"It's the pill," she told herself. "I've been taking it for far too long. It's a terribly powerful, unnatural drug, isn't it? No wonder my body's protesting. I'll stop taking it right away. Right away."

The period, which followed this decision, was fearful and immense. Gravity's claw reached up between her legs and pulled her insides out.

This was no ordinary curse. The truth could no longer be denied. Something was wrong with her body – but what? But what?

23

CHE GUEVARA'S HANDS

Monday morning, bright and early, Suzie retrieved Dr.Anton Cohen's card from her bag and telephoned him at his surgery in Highgate Village. She offered to buy him lunch.

They met in Hampstead at Le Cellier du Midi in Church Row.

In due course, after the first course, Suzie told him that she had a friend, about whom she was very worried.

Not for a moment did Anton believe that the friend in question was anyone other than Suzie. And Suzie knew he knew. But it was a convention, a corny convention, but useful nevertheless. It gave her room for manoeuvre.

"So then, this friend of yours – what are her symptoms?"

"She's got this bruising on her arms and legs. Her gums bleed. There's a pain, so she says, in her tummy. Her periods are appalling. And generally, apparently, she feels like shit."

"Where's the pain?"

"Which pain?"

"The abdominal pain."

"Here," said Suzie, and her hand went straight to the place where the pain was, even then, occurring. "At least, I think that's where she said."

"Upper left-hand side?"

"Is that significant?"

"It could be."

"Well?"

"Well what?"

"What do you think?"
"I think your friend should see a doctor."
"You're a doctor."
"She's not my patient."
"What would you do, if she was?"
"If she came to see me with those symptoms, in the first place I'd take some blood and send it off to be tested."
"For what?"
"I think I would probably wait for the tests to come back, before I'd be prepared to say."
"And if my friend refused to give her blood, until she knew what it was going to be tested for? What then?"
Anton shrugged, by way of a reply. His face was quite impassive. Suzie scrutinized it for some sign. He scrutinized her back, without pity, though the pity of it racked his very heart.
"Victor, I mean, Anton – sorry – I need to know what you think. I have to be able to tell this girl, this friend of mine ……. I have to be able to tell her ……. I have to ……. she's the kind of person who doesn't like going to the doctor," she ended, feebly.
"But she's sick. She has to go."
"How sick?"
"Maybe very sick."
"Put a name to it."
"Tell her to come and see me. Tell her to make an appointment. I'll see her any time she wants."
"Anton."
"Yes?"
"Put a name to it."
"Not until I've seen her."
This was the language of poker. It went with his poker face.
Suzie called him.

"We have to put a name to it. She's not the kind of person who'll come unless I do, until we do."

Anton laid his cards, carefully, on the table.

"The symptoms you described – the bruising on the arms and legs, the bleeding gums, abdominal pain, excessive periods, fatigue – are not inconsistent with the symptoms of leukaemia."

"Leukaemia," she echoed, tasting the word on her tongue.

"But it might be something else. It might be something quite benign. So, the sooner we get her in for tests, the better. Suzie? Do you understand?"

"Leukaemia."

As a word, it tasted liquid and cool. It was not an ugly word – a function of poetry perhaps, or some recondite figure of speech, like litotes or aposiopesis.

A waiter placed plates of some kind of food on their table. The waiter withdrew. Suzie stood up.

"I need the loo."

Anton waited a while, then he began to eat, with mechanical chews. What had he ordered? Liver? His appetite was shot to pieces.

When Suzie returned, her food was cold.

"Is everything alright?" their waiter wanted to know.

Suzie assured him everything was fine, but she seemed to have lost her appetite; then she looked at her watch and exclaimed: "My goodness, is that the time?"

She was late for a meeting in Tooting Bec, she claimed. She called for the bill. She had to go.

She paid and went, forestalling any further conversation.

If Dr Anton Cohen had ever entertained the thought of a fling with Suzie, the thought was now wholly banished. Like Monstro, Pinocchio's whale, sadness swallowed him whole.

"Leukaemia," Suzie read, in Mary Poppins' Pears Encyclopaedia. "This is a cancer of the white cells, in which the normal rate of production of any of the white cells gets out of control, leading to a pile-up of abnormal cells at the site of production (bone marrow, lymph nodes and spleen) or in the blood, or both. In spite of an increase in their numbers, their abnormality renders them unable to combat infection; sepsis and fever result. It is known that this kind of cancer can be caused by the effects of ionising radiation on the white-cell factory, and it is certain at least in animals, that viruses can also be responsible. Survivors from the atomic explosion in Japan have subsequently suffered from leukaemia far more commonly than the rest of us, as have doctors, nurses, and patients who have been over-exposed to X-rays. At the time of writing, leukaemia is still a uniformly fatal disease, although patients may sometimes survive many years. Their remaining time can nearly always be made more comfortable by various forms of treatment, and one day a cure will be found by research workers devoting their time to its study. It is difficult not to get very impatient with the slow progress of these studies, particularly when caring for children and young people whose lives are inevitably ended by the disease. The solution, however, as with other forms of cancer, probably depends on the understanding of the nature of life itself, and as long as biological research remains short of the relatively small amounts of money required to tackle these problems at speed, we have no right to be impatient, except with our elected leaders who spend far more than is needed on less important things."

"Oh, terrific," said Suzie to herself. "Now what the fuck do I do?"

The key phrases were: "uniformly fatal" and "probably depends on the understanding of the nature of life itself."

Oh yes? Is that all it depends on? Fat chance.

That night, Suzie had a dream, from which she awoke with a strangled scream.

"What's the matter?" Victor muttered, surfacing from sleep.

Suzie was sat up in the bed. She was drenched with sweat. She was massaging her throat, with obsessive, jerky motions, and staring straight ahead.

"I was having a nightmare," she said, in a small and strangled voice.

"Are you OK?"

"I dreamed that Che Guevara's hands were strangling me."

"Poor you."

"They weren't attached to his body."

"Disembodied hands, eh?"

"They cut off Che Guevara's hands."

"Who did?"

"The Bolivians. After they killed him. They cut off his hands and sent them to Castro in Cuba."

"What? Really?"

"It's a historical fact."

"I didn't know that."

"Only there was a mix-up in the post and, somehow or other, they sent Che Guevara's hands to me. I thought it was a birthday present, even though I knew it really wasn't my birthday. But somehow, in the dream, that made sense – so I opened the package, and Che Guevara's hands were inside, and they flew out of the box and tried to strangle me."

"Come here," said Victor.

He pulled her head down, gently, onto his chest. She snuggled into him.

"My God, you're soaking wet."

"I'm sorry."

"It doesn't matter. Sssssh."

He held her tight and, by degrees, her leaping heart calmed down, as he stroked away the furrows in her brow.

Sleep reclaimed her.

Victor, on the other hand, considering Che Guevara's hands, was suddenly wide awake. These severed revolutionary, anti-gravitational extremities seized his mind, applauded his genius, tickled his fancy, fondled his ego and, by means of intricate prestidigitation, conjured up his long-gone muse.

"Che Guevara's Hands".

Was that ever a title, or what?

Suzie's nightmare was Victor's inspiration.

And you know what? How about this for a novel idea, or in fact a non-novel idea? Because "Che Guevara's Hands" wouldn't even be a novel.

"Che Guevara's Hands" would be a play!

A two-hander!!

Hallelujah!!!

Victor had never written a play before, but, what the hell, if that bastard, Shakespeare, could do it, then so could he. So what, if Shakespeare's vocabulary was bigger than anyone else's? Big deal. Bard schmard. Shakespeare was a show-off. And Victor would show him.

"Che Guevara's Hands" would be the play to end all plays. He would make a fortune. Stars would stab each other in the back, fight duels, offer to have sex with him, hoping to appear in it. Suzie would come to the first night. She would be incredibly proud of him. Then they'd go home and make babies.

The following day, the rains came down, terminating the drought. Victor walked to work, beaming beneath his umbrella. It was perfectly clear to him that the drought in the land had been nothing less than a physical manifestation of the drought within his own creative kingdom. As day followed night, the ending of one signalled the ending of the other. Simple cause and effect.

24

SLAM!

Suzie picked up the phone and dialled Anton's number. She made an appointment. She went to his surgery in Highgate, opposite the cemetery where Karl Marx is interred. She dropped the pretence of an imaginary friend.

"I wish it was your friend," he said.

"I wouldn't wish this on any friend of mine."

"I mean, I wish it wasn't you."

"I know," said Suzie, gently.

She watched the needle into her vein. She watched the blood spring up into the syringe. She never looked away.

While waiting for the results, Suzie addressed herself to the business of buying Number Nine. The matter could be expedited promptly. Searches and surveys were not required. She knew the house. She wanted it – now more than ever.

The results came back.

"Doctor, doctor, how long have I got?

"Suzie, they're positive."

"No, no, no. That's not what you're supposed to say. You're supposed to say: 'Well, look at it this way, Mrs Blair, I wouldn't go out and buy any long-playing gramophone records if I were you.'"

"I'm sorry," said Anton, feeling utterly useless.

"Don't be sorry. Be funny. Give me a reason to laugh."

"I'm not very good at gallows humour."

"It's a damn sight better than gallows doom and gloom."

Anton said: "It's not completely hopeless."

"No?"

"The first thing we have to do," he soldiered on regardless, "is to get you into hospital."

"I don't want to go to hospital."

"Oh, but you must."

"Must I?"

"We have to do more tests."

"What kind of tests?"

"Tests to help us ascertain how to make your life more comfortable."

"What remains of my life."

Close your eyes. Imagine, you are thirty years old, and some poor bastard has just performed the most shitty of tasks: informing you of the fact that you are suffering from a disease for which there is no known cure. Hands up who has not imagined such a thing.

And hands up who has never sat around and discussed favourite and least favourite ways to die.

Short of being tortured to death for information which she did not possess, which was her most least favourite way to die, Suzie's second most least favourite way to die was falling apart by degrees, at the whim of some wasting disease.

Suzie's generation sang: "Hope I die before I get old." When Suzie was fifteen, it never even crossed her mind that she would live past twenty-one. When she was twenty-one, life beyond thirty seemed a remote and ridiculous impossibility. Once, at the Waitrose check-out, with her car illegally parked on the zigzag lines in Gloucester Road, Suzie had been waiting impatiently in line behind an ancient female shopper, who was taking forever finding her purse to pay for her one lonely apple, slice of ham and dented tin of Kat-o-Meat, reduced.

"Oh, for God's sake," Suzie snapped, "I hope I'm dead by the time I'm as old as you. You should have been put down years ago."

Schoolboys blithely prescribe global euthanasia for anyone over fifty. Then they grow up and become fifty themselves.

Suzie would not see fifty. She would not see forty. And, contemplating her imminent demise, she was, when it came to it, hard-pushed to see the difference between dying of leukaemia and being tortured to death for information which she did not possess.

"Why? Why me? Why are you doing this?" – This was the information they were after. These were the questions for which she had no answer.

"Tell us why we're doing this to you," the unseen torturers whispered in her veins, "and then, perhaps, we might stop doing this to you."

To be eaten at a gulp by a great white shark. To be flattened by a meteorite or some inconsiderate suicide, falling out of the blue. To be bitten by vipers, shot by snipers, or trampled to death by a herd of stampeding gnu. Anything was better than this, but this was all there was, because, well – well, because .... you tell me. I don't know.

"You're not planning to do anything stupid?" Anton wanted to know.

"Like what? Join the Moonies? Dye my hair green?"

"You know what I mean."

"Give me one good reason why I shouldn't."

"The longer you can live with a disease, the greater the chance we have of finding a cure, if not for you, then for someone else, a child maybe. Who knows? Every person who suffers contributes to the sum of our little understanding. To have a disease is to join in the fight against the disease. You could be the one .... you could be the one to give that vital clue. It's a terrible responsibility. But it's a responsibility that you now have."

"OK," said Suzie, absorbing this speech. She stared at Anton's carpet, a serious Turkey rug of brilliant muted hues. Then she raised her head and looked him in the eye. "Give me another reason."

"Well, there's your daughter."

"You think it's better for a child to stand by and watch her mother waste away in pain?"

Anton furrowed his handsome brow, searching for an answer.

Thinking of Jennifer, Suzie went on: "And do you think it's better for a mother to stand by and watch her child waste away in pain?"

Wasn't it Racine, or someone like that, who said that no tragedy is greater than that a parent should outlive her child?

"Pain can be controlled," said Anton. "Suzie, can't you see, even in the very face of death, our commitment has to be to life."

"What about life's commitment to me?" Suzie countered, angrily.

"You're angry."

"Wouldn't you be?"

"I probably would. But, hopefully, not with my family."

"I'm not angry with them. Haven't you been listening? I want to spare them. What's wrong with that?"

"Families have responsibilities too, you know."

"Meaning what?"

"Their responsibilities include loving you, come what may, in sickness and in health, no matter what kind of shape you're in."

"Don't they also have a duty to allow me to have the freedom to make the best death I can? How about that? God, this conversation is weird. I feel as though I'm in some stupid school debate, of a particularly boring kind. It's my life, and it's my death, and I shall do precisely as I please. What's it got to do with you?"

"Suzie, you came to see me," Anton reminded her, carefully.

"If I want to go out with a bang, I'll go out with a bang."

She snapped her fingers – SNAP! – and went.

Two days later, Suzie convened a family meeting.

George turned up with Wendy Green.

Suzie's first reaction was to ask George to ask the girl to leave. This was private family business. Then she thought: What the hell. She went into the kitchen, where Mary Poppins was feeding Jane with macaroni cheese.

Jennifer entered and wondered who this Wendy woman was.

"She's a cousin of Ronnie's. Works at the Beeb."

"Ronnie?"

"Tom's wife. You met her at the wedding?"

"Did I?"

"The cleavage," Mary Poppins sniffed.

"Oh yes. Oh dear."

"Come on, Mum, give the girl the benefit of the doubt."

"Oh I do, I do," said Jennifer. "Of course I do. And I'm very happy for George. Only I can't help thinking, a girl like that, she'll eat the poor boy for breakfast."

"Well, let's hope he enjoys it while she does."

"What's a cleavage?" Jane wanted to know.

"Don't talk with your mouth full," Mary Poppins scolded.

"It's the space between your bosoms," Suzie said.

"Don't be silly," Jane giggled. "I haven't got any bosoms."

Suzie remembered quite clearly the day that Jennifer bought her her first bra. She would never go shopping for bras with Jane. She would never …….. O, me! my heart, my rising heart!

The sound of Victor's key in the door told her that the time had come. The moment could no longer be postponed. Under her direction, they all adjourned to the dining-room.

Suzie sat at the head of the table. Jane sat on her left. Victor sat on her right. Jennifer sat next to Victor. Mary Poppins sat next to Jane. Side by side, at the table's other end, sat George and Wendy Green, holding hands.

It did not look to Jane as though there was any space at all between Wendy's bosoms, but never mind her bosoms, fascinating though they were. Apparently, this Wendy was going to eat Uncle George for breakfast! How exactly did she plan to do it? Would she boil him like an egg? Fry him like a sausage? Grill him like a kipper? Have him on toast? Or what?

"Right," said Suzie, "I'm going to make a speech, and I don't want any interruptions. I've thought about this long and hard, and what I'm about to say, maybe I should've told each of you separately, one by one – and maybe I shouldn't have told you at all, and kept it to myself. You'll just have to believe me, when I say, that on this particular occasion, I honestly believe that I owe you the truth. I really think I do. My intention is not to unburden myself at your expense. I would give anything for you all to be spared. But every time I try to work out an alternative course of action, I .... there doesn't seem to be any way round it."

Oh my God, wasn't this all a terrible a mistake? Couldn't she, even now, before it was too late, simply walk out of the door, climb into her car, put her foot down, and drive off into the Thames? Splash! Anton knew the truth. He could tell them why, when the ripples cleared.

Wendy stood up and excused herself: "I really don't think I should be here."

"I don't mind if you stay," said Suzie. "George will tell you anyway."

"No, I think I'll just wait in the other room, if that's alright with you."

Over George's protestations, Wendy left the room.

"Uncle George?" asked Jane, unable to contain herself any longer.

"Yes?"

"Is Wendy your girlfriend?"

"She is."

"And you're her boyfriend."

"That's right."

"So, it will be like not being able to have your cake and eat it, won't it?"

"What will?"

"When she eats you for breakfast!"

"Wendy's not going to eat me for breakfast."

"She is. She's going to make you into a lovely porgy porridge, and she's going to pour golden syrup all over you, and warm milk, and then she's going to gobble you up."

"Who says so?"

"Grandma."

Jennifer said: "Oh dear me. George, I'm sorry. I really am. I didn't mean it."

"Thanks ma," said George. "Thanks for the vote of confidence."

"Don't worry, Janie," said Victor, "if Wendy eats George for breakfast, we'll eat Wendy for breakfast. How about that?"

Jane thought this was an excellent idea.

"Hooray!" she cried. "Grilled Wendy and scrambled eggs! Bags I get the cleavage!"

"Jane!!"

Jennifer Perry and Mary Poppins expostulated in unison.

"And if there's any left-overs," Jane went on, giggling like a loony, "we can turn them into sandwiches and sell them in my shop."

"That's my girl," laughed Victor.

George stood up and glared at them.

"I see you've all been having a good laugh at my expense behind my back, as usual."

"George, do you mind? This is my show. Don't be such a Porge," said Suzie, who could not quite believe the way that things were turning out. This was supposed to be her big scene. She had had it all worked out, but somehow or other it seemed to be slipping away – like her life.

"No, I don't mind. I don't mind you ridiculing me. You've been doing it all my life. I'm used to it."

"George, that's not true," Jennifer protested.

"What I do mind, however, is you all having the nerve to ridicule Wendy, behind her back, and to my face. I can't believe it. It's inexcusable."

"Come off it, George, where's your sense of humour?" Victor wanted to know.

"I have no sense of humour where the woman I love is concerned."

"Woman you love?" scoffed Suzie. "You've only known her a week, if that."

"Well, I don't see what's wrong with that," said Victor. "We fell in love at first sight."

"Exactly," shouted George. "There you are. It's fine for Suzie, isn't it? But who cares what the stupid little Porge thinks? He's just a joke, isn't he? Ha ha, very funny. Well, let me tell you this ……."

"Sit down, George, there's a good boy," said Mary Poppins, sternly.

"I'm not your good boy, Mary. I'm a grown man. I'm a bloody millionaire, for God's sake. And I'm not staying here to be insulted.

So saying, George marched out, and slammed the door behind him.

Slam!

"Uncle George shouldn't say 'bloody'," Jane observed, cheerfully. "He's very naughty."

"George is a millionaire?" This was news to Victor.

Moments later, they heard the front door open and .... slam!

Suzie crossed to the large bay window, which looked out over the drive. She watched, as George crunched across the gravel, opened the Mercedes' passenger door, and ushered Wendy in. Slam went the door.

Slam!

George crunched round to the driver's side of the mighty automobile, climbed in behind the wheel, slammed his door.

Slam!

So many doors, slamming shut.

Slam! Slam! Slam! Slam! Slam!

Door after door after door after door.

No! Wait! Please, wait!

Too late. Too late.

At speed, the room receded into a tunnel.

The light at the end of the tunnel?

An on-coming train.

To the floor, to the floor, to the floor, to the floor.

Wham! Bam! Thank you, Ma'am!

Suzie fell to the floor.

25

BEYOND THE VALLEY OF SEX & SHOPPING

In an act of a stupendous folly, Tom had acquired, during the course of his South American honeymoon, a half pound of pure cocaine, which, having been secreted in a hollowed-out hard-back copy of Terra Nostra by Carlos Fuentes in the original Spanish, purchased in a book shop in La Paz, he mailed to himself at Thurloe Square. It had not yet arrived when he went to visit Suzie.

"How was it?" she asked.

"Brilliant," said Tom, perched on the end of her hospital bed. "Talk about mixing business with pleasure."

"Where were you exactly?"

"Peru, Colombia, Bolivia."

"Very nice."

"Hey, did you read about the plane crash in Santa Cruz?"

"No."

"Boeing 707. Thwack! Right in the middle of Santa Cruz. A hundred and two people – wiped out."

"Oh dear."

"We were right there. Fucking thing missed us by ten minutes. We were walking down the street, and suddenly Ronnie remembers she's left some stuff behind at the hotel, so we have to go back to get it. Ten minutes later, this motherfucker crashes right where we would've been, if Ronnie hadn't been so forgetful. How about that for karma?"

"Lucky you."
"Yeah. Lucky me."
"And not so lucky me."
"Listen, Suzie," said Tom, "I know you're, like, going to die. And I know it's a bummer ...."
"You could say that."
"But the thing is this – if it was me, I'd be thoroughly pissed off, if you turned up all miserable and depressed about it, coz, I mean, like, this is the gig, right? It's not as though you've got any choice in the matter. So, you have to make the best of it."
"I know that."
"Well of course you do. And the thing is, for what it's worth – you know what I believe?"
"What's that?"
"Or, rather, what I don't believe. I don't believe in death. Death is for dullards and dimwits, for people with small imaginations – not for the likes of us. Me? I'm an immortality man. I believe in the immortality of everything, yeah, in the immortality of atoms – the atoms of which a person is made. Suzie dies – a billion Suzies are born."
"Do you really believe that? Or is it just something you say?
"I believe that's what you ought to believe. OK, life is shit. Life is depressing. Read a newspaper. But the point is, you have to be optimistic – about life, and about death. It's a moral imperative. Know what I mean? It's an absolute duty. Zen and the art of living and dying. It's all the same thing. Thirty years. Sixty years. A hundred years even. In the face of infinity, for fuck's sake, life, however long, is no more than a blink of the eye. It's a blip on infinity's screen."
"Blip," said Suzie, with a sigh.
Tom laughed.
"What's so funny?"

"I was about to say: 'Don't give me any of your blip.'"

Suzie laughed too, really laughed, then winced, as the intravenous torturers decided it was time again to make their presence felt.

"It would be a whole lot easier," she said, "if there wasn't any pain."

"Pain can be controlled, my dear," said Tom. "We have the technology."

"They don't seem to have it here."

"Doctors don't know everything, you know. But I do have the wherewithal to cease upon the midnight with no pain."

"I like the sound of that."

Tom smiled at her.

"Well?" she said.

"Well what?"

"How would you do it?"

"Do what, Suzie?"

"Cease upon the midnight with no pain."

"Me? I'd swallow pure cocaine."

"To cease upon the midnight with cocaine?"

Tom loved that – to cease upon the midnight with cocaine.

"Now why didn't I think of that?" he said. "See, that's the difference between you and me. I know about poetry, but you, Suzie, you're an instinctive poet."

"How would you do it?"

They held each other's gaze for however long it was, during which time it occurred to Tom that this conversation was ceasing to be theoretical.

"Thomas?"

"I'd stuff it into capsules. Five grams, max, should do the trick. You swallow the capsules. The caps dissolve and – zing! – the big chill. Up and out with a smile on your face."

"Simple as that?"

"Well, you know me," said Tom, "per anything other than ardua ad astra. That's my motto."

"Tom?"

"Jawohl?"

"Would you do it for me?"

"What?"

"I want to cease upon the midnight with cocaine."

"Leave it to me," said Tom.

Strangely enough, Tom's copy of Terra Nostra, by Carlos Fuentes, in the original Spanish, was delivered to Thurloe Square even as this conversation was occurring.

Ronnie was out, when Tom got back from the hospital. She was buying cigarettes in Exhibition Road. Approaching the flat, she saw the bust go down. It was a combined Police and Customs operation. The boys from Customs and Excise can do more or less what they like. They do not need search warrants. Ring the bell? Why bother – when you're perfectly entitled to smash down the door? And that's what they were doing, smashing down the door. Ronnie did not hang about to see what happened next. She did not even break her stride. She crossed the road and walked away.

Karma? You better believe it. Fortune favours the lucky? You bet, until your lucks runs out. Cocaine? Class A drug. Maximum penalty? Fourteen years. But Tom never really thought those rules applied to him. Certainly not. Prison was dreadfully common. A place where criminals went. Tom was no criminal. An outlaw, certainly. But not a criminal. He was a gentleman. He saw himself as a gentleman outlaw purveyor of exotic pharmaceuticals to other discerning gentlemen outlaws with similar sophisticated tastes.

Against the advice of counsel, Tom made a speech:

"This is a question of fundamental civil liberties here .... whatever a man wants to do in the privacy of his own bloodstream .... if the law can't see the truth of this, the law is an ass ......"

And so on and so forth, until the Judge told him to shut up and sent him to prison.

Clang!

Slam!

The prison doors closed shut behind him, and there he was, Tom, beyond the valley of sex and shopping, facing a ten year stretch.

Suzie heard the news of his arrest from George, when George finally managed to extricate his penis from Wendy's cleavage, and appeared on the ward, bearing a bunch of grapes.

"So," said Suzie, "what brings you to this neck of the woods?"

"I brought some grapes."

"Thanks very much."

"I wanted to apologise."

"For what?"

"Well, you know, walking out like that the other day. I'm sorry."

"It doesn't matter. You had some justification."

"I'm still sorry."

"Everyone's sorry," said Suzie. "What can you do?"

George was sitting on a chair beside her bed, with his elbows resting on the blanket, when, suddenly, abject sorrow leapt out from the shadows and ambushed him. He buried his head in his hands and burst into tears.

"There, there, Porge," said Suzie, stroking the top of his head, "don't cry. There's nothing to cry about."

"I don't know how you can say that," snuffled George, fumbling for his hanky.

"From I where I sit, you get a kind of different perspective on things. Come on. Blow your nose. Have a grape."

"Thanks. Oh God," said George, stifling another sob, with

an inelegant splutter, "I just can't believe you're going to die." And he gave a monumental sigh.

"I'm not going to die. I'm immortal."

"Immortal?"

"Absolutely. Ask Tom."

"Tom's in prison."

Clang! Slam!

"I don't believe it."

"He's been busted."

"Oh shit. Oh dear."

"They've refused to give him bail. They're going to throw the book at him."

"Poor Tom."

"Poor Tom?"

"He's my best friend."

"He's been selling hard drugs."

"So what?"

"Hard drugs kill people."

"What do you know, Porge? People die of smoking every day. I don't see anyone rushing off and arresting Benson and Hedges."

"Listen, Suzie, I don't want to have an argument with you."

"Why not? Because I'm dying? Fuck it, Porge, my brain still works. Can't I even have a decent argument any more?"

"I'm sorry."

Suzie looked at George, shook her head and sighed.

"Just stop saying you're sorry," she said.

"I'll try."

"So, how's it all going with Wendy?"

"Oh, you know, very well," he said, and blushed.

Suzie laughed to see him go red.

"You're laughing at me." George began to bridle.

"Georgie boy, relax," said Suzie. "I'm very pleased for you. I really am."

"Suzie?"

"Yes?"

"Well, the thing is, I've done something, and I hope you're not going to be upset, but the thing is ……."

George ran out of steam, looked sheepish, reached for another grape, popped it into his mouth and chewed it in an ovine manner.

"Come on, George. What is it? Get it off your chest."

"It's about the house."

"Which house?"

"My house."

"What about it?"

"I've ….er ….. well ….. the thing is ….."

"Oh for goodness' sake, George, spit it out. The thing is what?"

"I've asked Wendy to decorate it for me, and I hope you don't mind."

"Why should I mind?"

"Well, I already asked you, and I wouldn't want you to think I was, you know, jumping the gun. I mean, Wendy wondered if it wouldn't maybe be better if we waited ….."

"What? Until I was dead and buried? How very tactful."

"You do mind."

"No, George, I don't mind. Honestly. Even if I wanted to do it, I wouldn't have the strength."

"Well that's what I said to Wendy."

"Oh yes?"

"And I also said that, if you didn't mind, it would be a really good idea for her to come and talk to you for advice. You know: builders, plumbers, painters, suppliers, all that kind of stuff."

"Tell her to look in the Yellow Pages, George. That's what I did."

"Oh," said George, taken aback.

"I don't want to have to think about inferior decoration any more. I've got enough on my plate as it is."

"So you do mind."

"George, read my lips. I – do – not – mind. How many times do I have to tell you?"

"What did she say?" asked Wendy, when George returned to the car, in which his beloved had been waiting down below.

"It's no skin off her nose."

"She doesn't mind?"

"She doesn't mind."

"And you don't mind?"

"Me? Mind what?" wondered George, his mind beginning to become confused with all this minding.

"Letting me loose on your house?"

"Well," swaggered George, preposterously, "if your taste in interior decoration is anywhere near as good as your taste in men, how could I possibly mind?"

As it happened, Wendy Green's taste was not in question. In fact, she had an excellent eye. Oh boy, did she ever have an excellent eye!

Paint? The fifteen shades of white were all bespoke and mixed by hand.

Bathrooms? Never mind the solid silver taps, ("Gold is so common, George."), the bidets imported from France, the shower-heads imported from a factory in up-state New York – there had not been so much excitement in Carrara, since dear old Michelangelo had got the locals hewing.

Rugs? She was particularly partial to large original Aubusson carpets.

Art? You had to have at least two Warhols. Owning one Warhol was nouveau riche. You had to have some Hockneys, but proper paintings. Lithographs were common. Jasper Johns? Put him in the kitchen. Rothko? Yes. In the card room.

Picasso? Pretentious in the drawing room, but perfect for the downstairs loo .... Get the picture?

From time to time, in fact frequently, in fact whenever he happened to be feeling horny, which was almost always nowadays, George would wonder: "Just how much is all this going to cost?"

"Now just you come here," Wendy would say, whenever George brought up the subject of money. Then, she would unbutton her blouse, unfasten her front-loading bra, which lifted and separated and divided – and, with a sure touch, reach for George's fly. And, somehow or other, the subject of money would sort of fade away, and fade away, and fade away ....

And then, one day, Black Monday, the day that eighty human beings died in Sydney in a train crash, the day that Gary Gilmore was finally shot, all George's chickens came home to roost.

His cheques began to bounce – all over the shop, which, in the first instance, was Asprey's, where Wendy had been hard at it, buying knives and forks. His credit cards ceased to function. The builders demanded cash, on the nail, or else. Then, to cap it all, the Inland Revenue decided it was time to take a long hard look at young Mr Perry's affairs,

George's affairs were in dreadful disarray – and it was all his fault. Much as he tried to blame his accountants, the sad truth was that George's accountants could scarcely have been anything other than incompetent, given the way he had been playing them off, incompetently, one against the other.

So, at the end of the day, George owed the taxman and, Jesus Christ, half of London, or so it seemed, more than he could pay.

They took everything away. The Mercedes, the house in Holland Park and all its contents, all his other properties, in Camberwell, Wimbledon, Chelsea, Chiswick, Wandsworth,

Battersea, Kentish Town. He went to the auction and watched, in limp disbelief, as his world was knocked down.

And so it was that Wendy Green seized George Perry by the penis and led him, like a lamb to the slaughter, beyond the valley of sex and shopping, to the place where bankrupts live.

Then she dumped him.

"I thought we were in love," George protested.

"Oh, grow up, George. Love is for children. What good is a bankrupt to me?"

A person with a cool head might come to the conclusion that, whatever the cost, George was lucky to be out of this particular relationship. George could not see it this way. The boy was in shock. Bankrupt. The very word filled him with dismay, never mind the fact that he had been taking advantage of people in the same position all his business life. It had, to him, a kind of shameful moral implication. It rhymed with corrupt. It was like wetting the bed.

He could have asked Jennifer for help. But he was far too ashamed. He could have asked Suzie for help, but how could he ask her for anything, when she was dying?

He went to Victoria, climbed on a train, and ended up in Brighton – and there was the sea.

26

BLOODY PETER PANIC

"Mummy?"

"Yes, darling?"

"Are you really going to die?"

"I'm afraid so, sweetheart."

"Now, Mummy, you mustn't be afraid. Well, maybe just a tiny little bit, because, really, it's very exciting, like in Peter Pan. Mary Poppins and me have been reading it again."

"Mary Poppins and I," Suzie corrected her, automatically.

"Yes, Mary Poppins and I, and, actually, Peter doesn't die, but he thinks he's going to die, and he's really very excited about it."

"Is he really?"

"Oh yes. He's a little bit afraid to begin with, but then, you see, he's very excited, because he realises that to die will be an awfully big adventure."

"It's the biggest adventure of all," Suzie agreed.

"Yes, I think it must be," said the solemn little girl, thinking ever so hard, her unlined brow furrowed with intense concentration. "But, Mummy?"

"Jane."

"When you die, who's going to look after me?"

"Grandma. Daddy. Mary Poppins. Uncle George. All the people who love you."

"But, Mummy, when you die .....?"

"Yes?"

"Will you have a funeral?"

"I certainly will."
"And will I be allowed to come?"
"Do you want to come?"
"Well, yes. But Daddy doesn't think I ought to come."
"How do you know that?"
"I heard him discussing it with Grandma. He thinks it might give me a trauma."
"Does he really? Well, don't you worry your head about that," said Suzie, marvelling, as ever, at the language of the child.
"Mummy?"
"What?"
"What is a trauma?"
"What do you think it is?"
"I don't know. Is it a kind of wart?"
"Not unlike. But it's an invisible one. And you get it inside, if you have a nasty shock. But you won't get one. I promise."
"Why not?"
"Because I love you too much."
From this moment on, the question of the funeral exercised Suzie's mind more than anything else.
"Now, Victor," she said, when Victor next came by, "let's talk about the funeral."
"Do we have to?"
"Absolutely. It's very important – for Jane."
"Suzie, she's only a little girl. She's too young."
"Nonsense," Suzie snapped. "She wants to come. I want her to come. I promised her she could come. And I promised her it would be fun."
"Fun? Are you crazy?"
"Victor, I want you to address your mind to the subject of my funeral. You're a creative genius. Do your stuff."
"Is this unbearable, or what? Suzie, don't you know how much I .... love you?"

"Don't, for God's sake, Victor, go schmaltzy on me now. I couldn't bear it. The funeral. Concentrate on the funeral. It has to be like .... the start of an awfully big adventure. Come on, Babe, I need your help. I can't do it without you. And if I don't get your help, I swear to God, the moment I die, I'll come right back and haunt you till you're blue in the fucking face."

"Alright. Alright already," he said. "I'll do my best. So ...... er ...... what do you want? Balloons?"

"Balloons! That's a great idea! Hundreds of balloons! Thousands of balloons! Filled with helium!"

"Oh yeah? So what are you going to do with them? Tie them to the coffin and float off into the blue?"

"Now THAT is a totally brilliant idea."

Despite his discomfort in this minefield of taboos, Victor could not help but grin with pleasure. On the whole, he was sadly lacking in praise for the things that went on in his mind. He was parched for praise. This was like water in the desert. Slowly, strangely, arranging the funeral became a kind of glorious, existential, death-defying-game. Like choosing their daughter's name, putting the fun into **fun**eral, gave them a kind of joy. Suzie and Victor were never so close.

"I think the coffin should be pink," she said.

"No – blue."

"What kind of blue?"

"Sky-blue."

"OK. Sky-blue."

"Where are we going to get a sky-blue coffin?"

"You can buy coffins. Buy a coffin and paint it. Get Jane to help. She loves painting things."

"Your mother won't like it."

Victor was absolutely right. Jennifer was horrified, aghast, and almost in total despair.

"I just simply cannot understand it. How could you even think of such a thing?"

"Mum, it's my funeral."

"Suzie," said her mother, stumbling through quagmires of pain, "how can you be so selfish? I mean, I'm sure you don't think you're being selfish, but surely, you must see, darling, funerals are for the living."

"I know that. That's the whole point. My funeral is for Jane. It's my last present."

"Suzie. I came back to the house and I went looking for Jane – and do you know where I found her?"

"No."

Jennifer had been out at the shops, and in the course of her shopping, she bought Jane a packet of Smarties. When she came home, she asked Mary Poppins where her grand-daughter was. They searched the house, high and low, and where did they finally find her? In the basement.

In the basement, lying in a coffin.

Lying in the coffin, which Victor'd had delivered, when everyone was out.

Lying, in the coffin, quite still, with her eyes shut.

Jennifer's heart had almost stopped then and there.

"Jane?" she said, barely able to hear her own voice, over the blood which roared in her ears.

"Hello, Grandma," Jane replied, not opening her eyes, in a funny distant voice.

"What are you doing?"

"I'm lying in Mummy's coffin," said Jane, in the long-suffering, patient voice you sometimes needed to use, when adults were being especially dense. "And my eyes are shut tight. And I'm imagining that I'm about to go off on an awfully big adventure."

Jennifer could have gladly strangled J.M. Barrie, and strangled Mary Poppins for reading him to Jane. But then, hadn't she herself read Peter Pan to Suzie, when Suzie was small?

When Victor had come home that evening, with a gallon of sky-blue gloss, Jennifer was ready to tear him apart, limb by limb.

"Listen, Jennifer, what can I do? You have to respect a dying person's wishes."

"Even if those wishes are totally wrong?"

"Who says they're totally wrong?"

"I do," said Jennifer, fixing him with a glare of absolute conviction.

"Listen, Mum," said Suzie, "I'm sorry if you got a bit of a shock."

"Bit of a shock! Suzie, use your brain. Imagine how you'd feel, if yours, God forbid, was the daughter who was dying."

"I wish no man harm," said Suzie. "I wish only to mitigate the pain and fear of dying – fear of flying – for you, for me, for Victor, and for Jane."

"Suzie, she was lying in your coffin, pretending to be dead!"

"Mum, children play. Rejoice in it."

"But when you come to man's estate, Suzie, when you grow up, you put off childish things."

"No! You don't!" Suzie countered fiercely. "Not if you want to be immortal. Not if death is really going to be an awfully big adventure."

"Bloody Peter Pan," Jennifer snapped in exasperation.

"What have you got against Peter Pan?" Suzie wanted to know.

"It's a children's story, Suzie, not the bible. I don't know, your whole generation, you seem to think that Peter Pan's some kind of moral philosophy."

Jennifer sighed, and shook her head.

"Suzie, you are not a child. You are a grown woman, with a

child of your own, with fearsome responsibilities, responsibilities I would give my very own life for you not to have to bear – but do you honestly believe that these terrible responsibilities make your immortal soul any the less immortal?"

Oh dear. Suzie had been dreading this moment. This moment that she knew was bound to come. This moment which would lead, inexorably, to the thorny subject of extreme unction.

If Suzie had ever harboured any lingering faith, as evinced in her disquiet, when it came to the business of not baptising Jane, her mind was now quite made up.

"By the way," said Jennifer, sidling into it, "I've been speaking to Father O'Day, and he'd like to come to see you."

"Why?"

"To hear your confession."

"Why?"

"Please, Suzie, don't do this to me."

"Why should I confess to him? What should I confess to him?"

"Suzie, darling, you mustn't die with sins upon your soul."

"What sins? I should apologise to God for what I've done? What have I done? What am I guilty of? Look at me! Look at me!! For Christ's sake, Mum, God should apologise to me."

Jennifer simply did not know how to respond to that.

Suzie went on, needing every ounce of her strength to focus on what she wanted to say.

"Listen," she said, "I'm sorry, but you can't have it both ways. If I'm a child, OK, you can treat me like a child. But if, as you say, I'm an adult, a grown woman, then, please, treat me as such. Respect my wishes. Allow me to meet my maker in my own way, on my own terms. Is that so much to ask?"

Suzie fell back on her hospital pillows, exhausted. She looked at her mother, and laughed, kindly.

"I'm glad you can laugh," said Jennifer.

"You should see the look on your face."

"The trouble is," said Jennifer, "whatever you say, you'll always be my child."

"Oh Mum," said Suzie, with a sleepy yawn, "I do love you very, very much."

Then she closed her eyes, and fell asleep, and in her sleep, some time later, died.

27

GRAVITY'S DOWNFALL

So ended the very worst day in Jennifer Perry's life.

It might, mind you, have been a whole lot worse, had not George, in Brighton, decided that suicide was not what he had been put on the earth to perform.

He had walked up and down on the beach quite a lot, kicking stones and pondering – pondering the case for walking into the sea and heading for France.

He had taken the lift to the top of the Metropole Hotel, gained access to the roof – and pondered jumping off it.

But, in the end, George came home, only to learn that Suzie was dead. His sister was dead. And in the midst of all the other myriad emotions, he could not help but think that, once again, the girl had stolen his thunder.

The coffin was painted sky-blue.

They placed the sky-blue coffin on the back of a chauffeur-driven flat-bed truck.

In the original plan, Suzie had wanted to commandeer George's Mercedes. But the Mercedes was no more. It was going-going-gone.

They tied to the side of the truck one hundred white helium-filled balloons, which danced and strained at their strings, eager for flight.

Victor and George and Jane sat on the back of the truck. Victor and George wore white suits. Jane wore her favourite dress, the dress she wore for poor Tom's wedding. Mary Poppins and Jennifer sat in the cab with the driver. Mary Poppins was dressed in Jaeger pink. Jennifer Perry wore black.

"I wouldn't presume to tell Suzie what to wear. And I assume that Suzie wouldn't presume to tell me," she said to Victor, when Victor mentioned that Suzie had wanted them all to wear joyful colours.

They set off on the route prescribed by Suzie, off on the final trip, round the landmarks of the town in which she once had lived.

Victor pressed play – and there was music, from the system he had rigged up on the truck.

Music!

As per Suzie's instructions, Victor had recorded a tape of the songs she wanted to hear inside her sky-blue coffin. (And he had sent a copy of this tape to Tom, who listened to the music on his Walkman in his cell. Tom's life and hers had been built on the back of these songs. They had always been stepping-stones to somewhere else.)

Impossible choices. For every one she put in, thirty, fifty, a hundred were left out. No Pink Floyd. No Dusty Springfield. No New Riders of the Purple Sage. No Aretha Franklin. No Velvet Underground. No Marvin Gaye. No Neil Young. No Frank Zappa. No Incredible String Band. No Ziggy Stardust. No Bob Marley. No Elvis. No time. No time. No time.

In the end, these were Suzie's terminal tracks:

"Key to the Highway" – Derek and the Dominoes – took them away from Number Nine, along the Lower Richmond Road, past the Food Shop, which was closed, and over Putney Bridge.

"Moonlight Mile" – Rolling Stones – took them down the New King's Road, passing people who waved and smiled, assuming them to be something wild, and certainly not a cortège.

"Dancing in the Street" – Martha and the Vandellas – and

"Red Neck Friend" – Jackson Browne – took them to Sloane Square.

"White Rabbit" – Jefferson Airplane – took them to Buckingham Palace, out of a window of which the Queen watched and wondered what on earth it all meant as The Beatles' "Revolution" bowled them along the Mall and up and through Admiralty Arch into Trafalgar Square.

"I Don't Want To (Hang Up My Rock n Roll Shoes)" – The Band – took them from Trafalgar Square to Fortnum's.

Bob Seger's "Get Out of Denver" was followed by Abba's "Chiquitita", taking them from Fortnum's to Harrods. Tom disapproved of Abba, but this was the only time that Mary Poppins' foot was seen to tap during the entire journey.

"Such A Night" – Dr John – and "My Ancestors" – Taj Mahal" – took them from Harrods to the Hogarth Roundabout.

Then "Brown Eyed Girl" – Van Morrison. This was for Jane, Suzie's special brown-eyed girl, and this was their special song.

And so they came to Mortlake Crematorium.

Mortlake. Lake of Death? Lack of Death? Lackey of Death? Lark of Death? Take your pick.

They carried the sky-blue coffin in, and, without benefit of any kind of clergy, though Jennifer prayed as hard as she could, underneath her breath, the coffin and its contents were committed to the flames.

Bob Zimmerman's heart-stopping "Forever Young" finished off the tape, and finished off Tom – and anyone else with half an ear to hear.

Waiting for the smoke, armed with scissors, Jane and Victor remained outside, on the flat-bed truck.

"There she is!" said Jane, bursting with excitement, waiting, ready with the scissors. "There she goes! Look! Quick! Goodbye, Mummy! Oh, Mummy, Goodbye!"

As the smoke rose from the chimney, into the early afternoon air, Jane and Victor snip-snip-snipped at the strings which held the hundred white balloons.

"Hooray!" cried Jane. "Hooray!"

This was gravity's downfall.

The white balloons ascended, scudding up the wind, chasing the smoke, into the sky-blue skies.

Beyond the valley of sex and shopping, eternity's playground lies.

28

UNCLE VANYA

Victor never did write his play.

What was the point – now that the person to whom he had planned to dedicate his work was gone?

Under Brigadier Perry's inscrutable eye, he packed up all his papers, into a cardboard box, and removed them to the basement; whereupon George, a new divan having been installed, moved back in.

By the terms of Suzie's will, Number Nine now belonged to Victor. So he found himself, for the first time in his life, in the unusual position of being a man of property.

George went to work in the Food Shop, where he put in long hours and kept his head down.

Despite Jennifer's determination that Jane should go to Benenden, where she insisted, correctly, that Suzie had been so happy, Jane, like her Uncle before her, refused point blank even to consider boarding school, so she went to Putney High, where she too kept her head down – and achieved middling results.

When Tom came out of prison, he found his world substantially changed. His father had died, leaving none of what remained of his money to Tom. His mother had sold the flat in Thurloe Square and moved to Monte Carlo with her judge. (Jennifer never did go to visit them in Oxford.) And Ronnie had instigated divorce proceedings the day he went inside. On his release, therefore, he was wifeless, homeless and broke.

To Tom's surprise, Victor came to his rescue: "I never liked you, you know that, Tom. But I know you were Suzie's best friend. I'm opening a new shop. There's a small flat above it."

"Oh. Where's that then?"

"White Hart Lane."

"I can't, like, afford to pay any rent."

"It comes with a job. You work in the shop."

"Oh, I don't know what to say, man."

"How about 'thank you'?"

Tom gave a small laugh and shook his head: "OK, Victor, thank you."

"You're welcome."

Someone had shaken the kaleidoscope. In the previous pattern, Victor had always seen himself as some kind of maverick element on the fringes of the arrangement. Now he found himself at the hub of the configuration, which, strangely, left him feeling more isolated.

An actress by the name of Karen Fox, who lived off White Hart Lane, and who came into the new shop, fell in love with Victor. She pursued him. Karen was very sweet, very charming, thought that Victor was absolutely terrific and, in next to no time at all, marriage was being discussed. Then he went with Jane to see her play Yeliena in Anton Chekhov's "Uncle Vanya" at the Orange Tree in Richmond.

By the interval, Victor was uncomfortable. What precisely was it about this play that was so spooky and unsettling? He could not put his finger on it.

Then, in the second half, he got it.

There they all were – on the stage!

An ancient nanny – Mary Poppins.

A doctor – Anton.

An old family friend who has fallen on hard times – Tom.

An old woman, whose daughter has died – Jennifer.

The old woman's son – George.

The old woman's grand-daughter – Jane.

The grand-daughter's father, husband of the daughter who had died – Victor himself.

And the grand-daughter's father's new wife, who is an actress, for God's sake!

Victor was beside himself with annoyance. Bastard Chekhov! How dare he? I mean, how dare he? I mean, it's one thing deciding not to write a play oneself, but it's quite another thing to find that you've, that you've, that someone has, that someone has somehow .... That someone has somehow what, Victor?

Well, one thing is certain. There is no way, no way, I can possibly even begin to consider marrying Karen now. I will not be manoeuvred into becoming a character in somebody else's play. I shall foil this fiendish attempt to take over my life.

Curtain.

"I thought we were going backstage," said Jane, as Victor marched out of the foyer and into the night.

"We're not," said Victor, who never explained to anyone, least of all to poor Karen, the reasoning behind his panicky retreat.

Confused and upset, not least because she assumed that Victor must have thought her a lousy actress, Karen ceased coming into the shop – and soon moved away from the area altogether.

The following spring, Jane was astonished when Victor announced that he was taking her on a trip to Eretz Yisrael.

"What?"

"Israel."

"Why?"

"To meet your grandparents."

It had taken him a week to track his ancient parents down, and now they were sitting at home in Tel Aviv and wondering what exactly it was that this errant son of theirs was after, after all this time – and hoping they would not die before he arrived.

Victor hated flying.

They were stuck in a stack over Lod, when some random turbulence, otherwise known as the hand of God, smacked into the side of the plane.

"Oh Christ," thought Victor, seizing his armrests with terror, and pushing himself back into the seat. His knuckles were white. His spectacles slid down his nose.

Jane gave him a pitying look.

"Hey, dad," said Jane.

"What?"

"What do you get if you take the **it** out of gravity?"

"You shouldn't make jokes about gravity, when you're sitting in a plane."

"Don't be silly. What do you get?"

"How should I know?" Victor snapped, gritting his teeth, over the engine's roar.

"What **do** you get, if you take the **it** out of gravity?"

"Gravy," Jane giggled, beaming from ear to ear.

Victor groaned.

"It's a joke, dad. You're supposed to laugh."

"I'll laugh when we land, if you don't mind."

But he smiled in spite of himself. Was this kid ever a chip off the old block – or what?

"Gravy," Victor muttered and shook his handsome head. "I wish your mum was here."

"Me too," said Jane.

She reached out to hold his hand, as the plane came in to land.

www.tablethirteenbooks.com